STREET KNOWLEDGE PUBLISHING

Published by: **Street Knowledge Publishing**
Street Knowledge Publishing
P.O. Box 345
Wilmington, DE 19899

Copyright date: 2016
ISBN: 978-1-944151-02-7

For The Love if It by K. D. Harris
Edited by Navimjan Services LLC
Cover design by Street Knowledge Publishing Services
Formatted by Krystol Diggs
Typed from handwriting to text by Vanessa Cooper

I0658877

www.streetknowledgepublishing.com

Printed in Canada

Asha

Chapter 1

"How much is it gonna cost for me to bust that thang open?"

I was turned off immediately. Ignorant ass comments like this, was one of the reasons I hated working these streets. Most of these dudes had no class, especially the young ones.

"Two-fifty...if you give up a few of them percs I'll drop it to two hundred." I paced back and forth scoping the area for the County boys. I didn't need them creeping up on me again. If I got popped this time I was going to Baylor's Correctional Institute.

"Are you serious?" He tilted his head to the left turning up his nose and chuckled. The look didn't do him any justice. He already looked like a blue-black Jay-Z.

"Nigga, ain't shit free in this world. I'm out here cause' I got bills to pay."

"Don't you live in East Bridge Projects?"

"What the hell does that got to do with anything?" I asked placing my hands on my hip.

3

"Bills! Bitch where...," he laughed as if he told the best joke on earth. I rolled my eyes in disgust. "Your rent prolly like five dollars."

There were many insulting thoughts running through my mind. His dusty ass was lucky that I would *even* allow him to sniff my prized pussy.

"Time is money and right now you're waistin' my time which means you're fuckin' with my money." I was tired of the Joe type behavior. I was missing out on real money entertaining this lame.

"You talk real heavy to be a Hoe. I ain't giving your thot ass shit; you better take these percs and handle your business!" He leaned against his dingy white Chevy Impala grinning like he was hot shit.

I smiled coolly. He was about to be in for the surprise of his life. I definitely was in need of my "meds"; however, I wasn't about to put his funky balls or allow his diseased dick in my shit for only ten fuckin' percs. This dude was drawin'.

"You know what...I'm good. I don't give up my goods for pills only, you better head on over West and see Phyllis and Black Suzy. Percs don't pay my bills baby. No cash-No ass-period!" I began to walk in the other direction in search of another trick. My neck jolted backwards, he took a fist full of my weave and pushed my head to the side with force. I swore I felt my shit snap.

"Fuck you then you EBT, pill poppin' thot box! Get the fuck on your knees you gon' suck this dick, Hoe."

I tried to break from the grip he had on my hair. The burning sensation in my neck caused the fighter in me to awaken. His grip was firm. My three hundred dollars of Brazilian bundle hair was wound up around his fist like a wad of toilet tissue. I had two choices: one, let this nigga whoop my ass and suck his dirty dick or two, break free and lose some hair. I chose the latter. He was *too* disrespectful and needed to be handled.

I played it cool.

"Ok nigga, I'm coolin' let go of my hair and we can do this," I lied.

Like a sucker I knew he was, he did as I requested. I scanned the area and found my weapon of choice - an empty *Ciroc* bottle that lay at my feet. I swiftly took hold of it and bashed him on the side of his head with every inch of strength I had in me. As soon as I made the connection I didn't wait to see what the outcome would be. I took off like a track star in five inch stiletto heels. I heard him shouting in the background and never looked back. I headed towards an abandoned house in Hamilton Park. I didn't break my stride until I entered the broken back door. Once inside I peeked through a hole in the boarded up window. I watched him hop in his whip and peel off leaving a mass of thick black smoke in the air as he headed towards the Eden Park.

I took a seat on the wooden chipped-up counter top. *This shit is for the birds*. This was the third time this week somebody tried to get over on me. The other girls on the Ave had pimps. The pimp thing wasn't for me. If I was the one spreading my legs, no one would reap the benefits but me. I never understood the logic. To be honest most pimps treated their girls like trash. No one was clad in high class attire. They wore cheap Rainbow sets or the outfits they sold out the Chinese store on Market Street mall or not to mention the ever so popular Cowtown specials. I was a prostitute but I had pride in myself.

I took ten minutes to rest before heading back to my post. There was money to be made and I couldn't afford to miss out on it. I worked the corner of Terminal and New East Avenue, affectionately known as *Cash Ave*. The same spot my Auntie Lynn, had worked. Her twin sister Netta had also worked on the avenue closer to the Rosegate area. All of the females in my immediate family had ties to the oldest profession recorded; thanks to Aunt Lynn. She made it look glamorous. I didn't choose this life. It chose me. Whoring was in my DNA. It's the reason why I never wanted any children of my own. They say the apple didn't fall far from the tree. In our case we created a bushel of those apples. We were cursed. My intentions were to be the complete opposite. Unfortunately, it didn't pan out that way. Like the others, I was considered to be a prostitute, a whore, or as the young people call it, thot. I was a woman who made a living lying on her back with her legs, mouth, or ass available for a nigga or bitch to get their rocks off; for a *fee* of course. I tried to take a different approach; I considered myself a business woman and carried myself as such...at least I thought I did.

My Aunt Lynn conducted most of her business on the Ave; however, on occasion she would invite a trick to our crib on B Street. The bounce of her bed screeching across the jail house tiled floor would awaken me out of my sleep in the middle of the night. I would remain up, staring at the ceiling until the brilliant rays of the sun snuck through the rips in the shade which covered my bedroom window. This went on before I was old enough to know what trickin' was and continued after I discovered its' true meaning. I would run to the bus stop, eager to go to school to escape my problems at home. In class, is where I found my rest...unfortunately the teachers didn't appreciate me using my desk as my bed. I ended up dropping out of high school and soon figured out that without a high school diploma my career options were limited to bagging groceries at *Shop Rite* or working at some chinks hair store selling five dollar weave. I wasn't with none of that.

7

I ended up going back to get my diploma by attending Job Corp in Keystone, Pennsylvania. I earned my CNA- Certified Nursing Assistant License. I bounced around a few nursing homes for a few years. The money was only good if I worked overtime. I ended up getting in a car accident and was unable to go back to work. I was mad yet relieved; I realized wiping old people's ass was not the look-at least it wasn't for me. Besides, I was missing out on all the good parties. I ended up settling out for ten thousand dollars from my lawsuit. At least that's what I walked away with after all the medical bills and my bullshit lawyer was paid. Everyone said I should have gotten a better lawyer. When it first happened no one was throwing legal advice my way. My plan was to use the money I received to move out of the projects. I was headed to the suburbs, however that never happened; my stash was gone within two months from shopping. Without my PIP money I had to pay out of pocket for my narcotics - which I had become addicted to even though I refused to admit it.

In a matter of months, I was dead broke. Desperate for fast cash, I reluctantly entered my Auntie's profession. I started out with the rap stars, party promoters and the plugs; truth be told majority of them was popping pills too. A few tried to wife a bitch up, but I wasn't about that. I was all about getting my next high and doing me. Half of those niggas I had laid up with fucked at least one of my family members, they weren't really about shit. I soon wore out my welcome amongst the elite so Aunt Lynn turned me on to the Ave. We were the hottest bitches out there. Our fuck game was so on point niggas was spending so much money you would have thought they had holes in their pockets. Our pussy put a spell on these dudes and we ran through them like water down a pregnant bitch's leg. We had the game on lock-that is until they found her body sliced in diced on a bench in Braggs Park. My Aunt Netta was shook; so shook up that she ran to the church house and never looked back. She was now a first lady of some mega preacher that was on TBN in Memphis. I on the other hand didn't know how to feel; I was happy that she was out of my life, but I couldn't help to wonder…why now? God could have snatched her out of here years ago. Maybe Netta, I or my other young cousins would have never set foot on the Ave.

I chilled out and found me a dude they called "Cream" from the South Bridge Projects. He was black as tar; the nickname was not fitting in the least bit. He would always pull up on my post and tell me how I was too pretty to be throwing my life away. He was on some captain save-a-hoe shit. Thing was I didn't want to be saved...at least not by him. I would never pay him any mind, cause he was a half ass hustler selling coke for the blind lady that lived out in New Castle. I could never understand how he was hustling *for* her. How the fuck she ain't know if people were robbing her for her shit or not? The crazy thing is these mother fuckers were scared to death of her like she as some *monster* type Queen Pen. I found that shit laughable.

I ended up inheriting my Aunt Lynn's' project house. He ended up moving in with me.
Things were cool for the most part, he made sure I got my pills and I made sure his stomach stayed full and his dick satisfied. He had this mutt Bitch that tried to act up. I ignored her most of the time. After a while I became bored of it. I needed my own money. He got a little job at the docks and I started calling up my old sugar daddies to pick me in front of K&F. I figured if I kept the same clients I would make money and be safe.

This one day it was hot as hell outside. I received a text from one of my regulars. I told him to meet me at the store. I wore a Lily white linen sleeveless shirt-styled dress that I picked up on clearance at Macy's and a cute pair of gold Steve Madden gladiator sandals. As I stated before, I may have been a hoe but I was classy with my shit.

I stopped in the store and grabbed a Mango Arizona tea to quench my thirst. In the midst of gulping down my drink like a man, I noticed a fly ass black Range Rover pull up in front of me. I knew by the body type it was the latest model out. I was absolutely in love with the vehicle. It was bold, regal and damn right sexy as shit. Which meant the owner possessed something I loved...money.

The window from the passenger slid down. I was seduced by the sound of Teja Seville's 'Love is Contagious' that song was old as shit. I remembered it because my mom used to sing it all the time to my dad. I rarely heard that song, but when I did it brought me great joy which was shortly followed by depression. I knew this wasn't my trick but I was drawn to the car. I strutted over and leaned in the window to greet him. I paused in shock when I saw the gorgeous creature that was behind the steering wheel. A man this fine was only in the movies. Last time I checked, my life was real as shit and we weren't in Hollywood. *He has to be lost. I know damn well he ain't from 'round here.* I thought.

"What's up," I said, giving him my most seductive smile. He was dark skin with a reddish tint with a low cut around the sides and a sea of waves on top of his head. He was so wavy he needed to be on an atlas. His shape-up was precise. *He must be a sand nigga.* He was probably related to the Arabs that owned K&F or the ones that ran the BP gas station. I checked him over once more and he was dripping in ice. *This nigga is caked up!* Sand nigga or not I had to have him. Shit it wouldn't be the first time I fucked a trick out of my race. *Wait a minute. Hold on Asha, he might not even*

11

be on that type time. His dress game was on point. I knew it was designer but there were no names visible. Our people tended to be label whores.

"Hey Love," swag slivered through this dude's perfect lips, they weren't plump nor were they thin. They were just right. *Who was he and where did he come from?*

"Is there a hotel nearby?"

Hotel? Don't tell me this nigga is a trick for real.

"If you go downtown we have plenty, I believe the Hotel Dupont will suite you fine," I said. "Turn right at this corner and keep over the bridge and you'll be downtown."

He looked me over for a moment before speaking. "Since you know what will suite me, how about you come in and show me how to get there? He suggested with a sly grin.

So he is a trick. I laughed to myself. *It was too good to be true.* I opened the door and slammed it shut. He kept his eyes on me the entire time.

"Five hundred and for an hour you can fuck me until my insides fall out." I kept my head turned towards the window. For some reason I was feeling some type way but I wasn't sure why, though.

"Whatever you want love," he replied and pulled off.

"My name is Blair. And you are?" He asked, steering the steering wheel with one arm and playing with his radio with the other.

Blair. He didn't look like a Blair. I thought he would say Muhammad, Amed or some shit. Blair was rich and sexy as shit, why he was trickin' was beside me. He could have some high priced model chick on his arm. I couldn't help but think of ways to put it on this nigga so I could drain, let me rephrase that, send a drought to his bank account. Without thinking I said, "Asha...Asha Thomas," I wanted to slap the shit out of myself. I just told this dude my government name. I was on some dumb shit. Shit, maybe this wasn't a good idea. This nigga was able to get information that no other trick that I didn't go to school with was ever able to find out.

"That song you were playing reminds me of my parents. They were killed when I was twelve."

"I'm sorry to hear that love. It must have been rough losing your parents at a young age."

"Yeah, rough." I snorted.

Silence.

"Go ahead and laugh," I said. "I'm fucked up, I know."

Blair responded with a warm smile, but he didn't laugh. "You can't control the hand you were dealt love, however you can change the way you play it. I would never laugh at another's suffering.

We rode in silence the rest of the way of the hotel.

I waited in the car while he went inside to pay for the hotel room. He returned and handed his keys to the Valet driver. We entered into the grand hotel. The lobby was breath taking. I had been here only one time before with one of my Aunt Lynn's clients. He was an old white man who liked for us to take turns beating his ass. We never fucked him; we just pulled on his little pink dick and beat his ass with sex whips. He was on some whole other shit, but he paid great. We rode the elevator to the fourth floor and went to room 412. As soon as we stepped foot inside of the hotel room, I pulled the straps off of my shoulders and let the dress fall to the floor. I stepped out of it, turned to him unsnapped my bra and ran my hands across my curvaceous size nine body.

"Nice."

Nice tho-really? My body has been called a lot of things; sexy, stacked, banging and some more shit. I ain't ever heard my shit described as *nice.*

Blair slowly walked towards me and picked up dress then handed it to me.

"What?" I held the dress in my hand baffled.

"Get dressed." He sat on the side of the bed watching my every move.

"Look…I'm not sure what is going on but the clock is ticking boo,"

"You'll get your money."

I shrugged my shoulders and put my dress back on. I went over to the bed and lay back. He gently placed my hand in his.

"Why do you behave like this?"

I thought we already went over this shit in the car. He was blowin' me. "I get paid to behave this way?"

Silence.

I sat up in the bed. "How am I supposed to behave? I sell my ass for money. What am I supposed to be garbed up?"

He laughed.

"Why do you continue to do what you do?"

"Oh my God! What you Fifty Cent now, what's up with twenty-one questions?" I jumped up from the bed. I was uncomfortable. "Are we fucking or what cause if we not give me my five and I'm out. I can find my own way home!"

"Is it so hard for you to believe that a man might just enjoy being in your company? I just want to talk...get to know you."

"What is there to know? I told you more than you needed to know already. Nigga my degree is in fuckology not psychology." He sat there with a blasé expression. "I gotta go." I stuck my hand out, palm up in his face. I was beyond agitated. I didn't know what type time he was on but I wasn't feeling it. He could have been an undercover cop for all I knew.

Blair reached into his pocket and pulled out a wad of money. He peeled off ten hundred dollar bills and handed them to me.

"Keep some of it on tuck before you hand it over to your pimp?"

"Pimp?" He was trippin', this ain't the movie Friday and my name damn sure ain't Darla. "I work for myself, I'm self-made…."

"So, you can quit at any time?"

I rolled my eyes and turned back to him. I could feel him watching me as I exited the door.

This was the first time I left from a hotel with a nigga I ain't fuck even after I was paid. Tears escaped my eyes. I became angry. He made me feel something I hadn't felt in a long time - *conviction*.

Shonni

Chapter 2

Click. A bright light flashed from my iphone 6s as I took a picture of the fresh tropical blonde Bamboo floors that had been laid on my entire first floor. I couldn't wait to receive the rest of the items for my "living space" from Bassett Furniture. I slipped on my Gucci flip-flops and went into my small kitchen and took a seat at my bistro styled table for three. I tapped the *Snap Chat* app on my phone and cropped out the picture I took of the floors. Even though I lived in the projects, I refused to live the life of a destitute person. I learned how to use my assets as a bartering tool to gain the finer things in life, I refused to work myself to death for them. Last time I looked in the mirror, I wasn't my mother she worked three jobs and we were still barely making it.

I grew up in the heart of West Baltimore; in the most crime and rat infested area. We lived in a three bedroom row home with four cracked white stone steps leading to the entrance. I remember sitting on those steps daily plotting my escape from the horrific place. I was the oldest of five children and was always left to be in charge of my younger siblings. I was the mother, the father, the maid and the chef. At the age of sixteen I turned in my resignation and made my escape. My mother's check had come in the mail from one of her many jobs. I took the check and went to the corner store and cashed it. I was seven hundred thirty-five dollars and twenty-six cent rich. I caught the bus to the greyhound station and bought a ticket to Wilmington, Delaware and hadn't looked back since. That was eight years ago.

***

Three hours later...

I sighed heavy, picked up my phone and told Siri, "Call the office."

The phone rang four times before it was picked up.

"Mayor's office could you hold please?" I didn't even get a chance to say anything. The music playing in my ear was a soft jazz tune. I began humming along with it before being interrupted by Neil's dippy secretary.

"Mayor Santoki's office. How can I help you?"

"Kim, put Neil on the phone,"

I heard her smack her lips, "Mayor Santoki is in a meeting. May I take a message?"

"Remind Mayor Santoki that it's *election time-* thank you."

I heard her gasp in disgust. "Hold please."

The next voice I heard was Neil's. He didn't even acknowledge me. "What's the problem?"

"My furniture was supposed to be delivered at noon and it's now 3:20 and it's still not here."

"You're interrupting my meeting for, this?"

"Neil, don't act like that. You know the deal, I take care of you and you make life great for me. Now, either you hold up your end of the bargain or the News Journal may find out about your three illegitimate children and mistress you keep hidden in East Bridge projects. I don't think the city will like that you're using city funds to cover up your secrets."

"Hold on," Neil said, obviously frustrated and annoyed. "She is starting to act just like those other ghetto bitches..." I heard him say under his breath before clicking over.

Wow, is that how he feels?

He clicked back over "It will be there shortly. I don't ever want to hear you threaten me with *those* kids again. If you do, you'll be sorry."

"That's not a problem. Just make sure I have my items to me by five o'clock today or you'll more than likely find your face plastered across Delawareonline-.com and in divorce court." I ended the call. I'm sure he understood what was up.

Home wrecker, slut, tramp, scandalous, trifling—I had been called everything under the sun outside of a child of God. *Just jealous ass broads tryin' to knock my hustle.* People were quick to pass judgment on the next person without considering all of the factors involved; there was always a reason at the root of every problem. Neil was my sponsor since I arrived in Wilmington. As a matter of fact he was the first person I met. I had just gotten off the Greyhound. It was cold outside and it hit me that I had nowhere to go. I wandered around the Market Street Mall until it got dark. There was a Double Tree hotel on the corner. I decided to try my luck at getting a room there. I pulled my hair out of the pony tail, brushing it towards my face hoping it would make me appear older. I walked inside, I paused before approaching the desk. I did a quick scan to see who I would target first. There was a young black guy to my right and two older white women to the left. I chose the left. Ten minutes later I was walking away with a room key. It wasn't until I was on the sixth floor that I realize I was being followed by a brown skin man dressed professionally. I turned around, "Can I help you?"

"No, but I can help you." He said, in a smooth voice. I was confused. He took me by the arm taking the key from me. I tried to run because I thought he was the cops. He told me to calm down and that he wanted talk. He told me his name as Neil Santoki and he worked in the mayor's office. He went on to say that he had been following me since I left the bus station. I thought that was creepy. He continued on saying that I had a beauty that was rare and he knew I didn't belong here. He ended up taking me under his wing and two months later I was pregnant with our first child. He pulled some strings and got me a place in a newly built housing project called East Bridge. I looked at him as my savior. He provided all of my needs as long as I promised not to mingle with the other residents. He made me feel like I was better than them. He took me to art shows, museums out of state and taught me about the finer things in life. I thought that one day he would take me away from here to be his wife. I didn't know he was thirty-nine and married until after he became mayor. He paraded his plump blonde hair blue-eyed wife and their three pre-teenage children. That blew me.

At exactly four in the afternoon, a Bassett truck pulled up in front of my unit. I went to the door.

"We got a delivery for a Shon Anderson. Sorry we're late, it's been a busy day," the short stocky one said, handing me a clipboard to sign for the delivery.

"And it's hot as hell out here," said the tall lanky one.

Physically, neither one of them were bad looking. Financially, they were declared unfit.

I rubbed my hand over my new couch. It was as soft as butter. My body melted into the cushions when I sat down. The new end tables and coffee table that another "sponsor" of mine had purchased for me two weeks prior coordinated perfectly with the couch. I admired my living space décor: My walls were painted a light sea foam green; A twenty-two by thirty-four Gamboa, Consuelo original entitled "Giclee" rested above my chaise; The other wall was covered by an Oak cabinet holding my forty inch Sony Plasma Smart Flat screen television...courtesy of my children's father and number one sponsor, the Mayor.

Looking around my unit, I had everything I wanted and yet it wasn't enough. I stared at the one-year-old Plasma TV. It still looked brand new. *It's time to go bigger*. My cell phone rang.

"Hey, baby, I was just thinkin' about you," I lied.

"I'm glad to hear that because I *need* to see you tonight." Dominic stressed the word need as if he was running low on air and the only supply of oxygen on Earth was buried deep in the mine between my legs.

"The door will be open," I said, hitting the end button on my phone.

Neil was the mayor. Dominic Massea was high powered criminal defense attorney. I met him about a year ago. I was leaving out of the Carvel State building after sucking the Mayors stress away. I was so busy checking my make-up that I didn't see the wet floor sign. I slipped and before I could hit the ground he caught me. I lay scantily dressed in his arms. But the first thing I noticed was the rose gold Patek Philippe on his tan wrist. *Damn.* I knew I had to bag him. I hadn't even seen his face - the sunburst brown one on his wrist was enough.

"Are you ok?" he asked.

"Oww-ouch...," I pointed to my perfectly fine ankle, "I-I think I broke it." I moaned.

He chuckled. "I doubt it," He lifted me up, "You can't sue anyway there's a wet floor sign and cameras all around." He pointed out.

I blushed in embarrassment, he pulled my card but he was cool about it. I looked him over. He was dressed in a black suit with a silk mauve tie. His cufflinks and shoes screamed *wealth*. When I finally looked at his face, I knew exactly who he was. His face was plastered across every major news channel; He was the golden child of crooked ass Judge William Massea. Neil could not stand them. He swore they were connected to the mob. It was rumored that William might enter as an candidate for mayor this upcoming election. Neil was scared as shit because unlike him, the Masseas were for the black people and would most likely win.

His sea blue eyes sparkled as he lusted over me. I wasn't surprised. My beauty as well as my cunning characteristics had that effect on men.

"My name is Shon Anderson," I said, imitating the man stealing women from the frequent life time movies I studied. You know the ones about the women who scheme their way into politicians' beds.

He shook my hand an introduced himself. We shared a few laughs and he gave me his card.

Two days later we were in his office located across from the court fucking like wild dogs. After a week I had him stuck. He promised to provide for me with one restriction—that I didn't sleep with anyone else. He had a lot of nerve. He was a married man with a whole family he toted around in the public. He was only six years older than me unlike Neil who was damn near in his mid-forties. Nic and I had more fun together. He was a cool ass white boy, and his dick wasn't bad either. I allowed him to believe he was my one and only. For my obedience I received a bi-weekly check of two thousand dollars.

* * *

Scented candles burning in every room, a path of red rose pedals leading to my bedroom, and a tray of strawberries, chocolate syrup and whip cream ready to serve before the main entree. Tonight I was hoping he would say yes to buying me a new flat screen TV; not that I needed it.

In and out. In and out. I squeezed my vagina muscles, trying to tighten up my shit before Nic showed up. Usually, he was none the wiser and had only questioned me once…hours before he came I was receiving the dick down of the century from, Man-

Man or Manson as I call him. He was a major dope supplier and a faithful client of Nic's. I met him one day in Nic's office when I was filling in for his secretary. He was dropping off a large cash retainer for Nic's services and we ended up leaving at the same time. Five minutes later he was hitting it from the back of his Escalade; I swear it was the best dick I ever had. I hadn't even planned on getting money from him. But he hit me off with a stack and I been fucking him damn near every day since.

Headlights shined through my blinds and seconds later there was a knock on my door.

Didn't I tell his ass that it would be open? I tightened the belt around the maroon, silk robe I had on and switched to the door causing my ass to jiggle. It wasn't Nic. It was Dale, his accountant.

Carly

Chapter 3

She glared at me from the moment I hopped on the Dart bus, rolling her eyes and making snide comments under her breath. *If she looks at me one more time...*She looked.

"What's your fuckin' problem?"

The other bus riders looked on, anticipating the argument to come. Several turned the volume down on their electronic devices while others halted their conversations completely or looked up from their reading materials. All eyes were now on her as everyone waited for her response, including me with a *bitch fight me* stare on my face.

"White bitches like you tryna be black is my problem..."

People kill me with that bullshit. I had been living in South Bridge—surrounded by a majority of black people—since I was three-years-old.

"Bye Felicia. Go 'head somewhere with your raggedy ass!"

"Just triflin'."

"And you dusty...'

The bus stopped. *Good.* I was done arguing.

The Department of Human Services commonly known as the welfare office was a block up from the bus stop. This place was like a second home to me since I could remember. I was told we once lived in suburbs in a big house with my father. My mother fucked it up when my sister came out too dark with thick coiled hair. My father left her at the hospital and me at daycare and was never seen again. I guess the thought of a black man laying with his wife was too much. We stayed with my grandmother for a while but when Nola started to get darker and resemble her father's side we had to go. We ended up in the Hope House shelter and the counselor signed my mother up for public housing. We were supposed to move to Riverside projects but something opened up in South Bridge instead.

Very few rolled out the welcome mat when I first stepped foot in the projects. I was called all kinds of names from wanna-be, white-trash-hunky and whatever other insult they could think of. My mom was not used to living this way, she eventually fell victim to the system and started smoking crack. Two more siblings were added to the clan. At the tender age of thirteen I added my own addition to the family a son named Syncere; three years later I had my daughter

Synda and last year I had Symia. Their father was, Symai aka Cream. He got the nickname because he had wifed up a white girl, me. He lived over in East Bridge with some thot named, Asha. I couldn't stand that bitch. I had no idea why he wanted to be with a bitch who sold her ass for a living.

I walked the distance to DHS. It wasn't even nine o'clock in the morning and the waiting area was packed, there used to be a time when you would see only women here, now there were men, *young* men at that, trying get a slice of the welfare pie.

"How many appointments does Mrs. Davis have before mine," I asked the clerk as I signed in.

"Six."

"Six!" *Damn it. I don't feel like bein' up in here all day long.* The afternoon before, I had received a letter in the mail stating that my benefits were being discontinued. The little assistance that I did receive from the government was the only source of income I had coming in—not counting the money I got on the side selling Xanax and Percocet. My Uncle Henry, my mom's brother was a doctor. I started going to him last year as a patient, he didn't agree on how we were treated so he gave me prescriptions every month to take care of my family. It's amazing the lengths people would go to cover their guilt. I made close to fifteen hundred a month, but that was nothing when I had three kids plus my two younger siblings to look out for.

"Carly Felton."

I looked up to see Mrs. Davis calling my name. *I thought I had six people ahead of me.* I wasn't going to question her. I got up and followed her. She was my latest caseworker. The others had quit, complaining that they were overworked and underpaid. She was an older light-skin woman with long brown hair. She gestured for me to take a seat in her crowded, overstuffed and small cubicle. *Glad I'm not closter-phobic.* Case files were piled in stacks, high on her floor. Her desk was buried underneath more case files and paperwork stained with splashes of coffee.

"How've you been, Ms. Felton?"

"Better before I got this in the mail." I gripped the letter in my hands. "It says my benefits are going to be cut off."

"Yes."

"Why?"

"I think you know the answer."

"No, I don't."

"Ms. Felton, we have cause to believe that you've been letting other people use your EBT card in exchange for cash. Your case file is under fraud investigation."

"What? That's ridiculous."

"It may be but in the meantime, your benefits are being discontinued."

"This is some bullshit." I rolled my eyes.

The truth was that I *was* guilty. Besides selling pills I had been selling my mom's stamps to get extra money.

"Calm down, Ms. Felton." She said, adjusting her glasses.

"How the hell am I supposed to calm down when I don't know how I'm going' to feed my children?" I asked, still upset.

"I'm sure you'll figure out a way." She said, emotionless.

I stormed out her office slamming the door. When I got out into the hallway, I couldn't believe my eyes. That bitch Asha was standing by the water fountain with Zoe, Cream's older sister. They looked at me then looked at each other and laughed.

"Fuck you, you fat nasty bitch!" I shouted.

Zoe laughed harder, "Ooh-she mad!" she teased.

I was furious I wanted to smash her swollen face in to the wall. Asha smirked, eyeing me like she was about to do something.

"What Bitch?" I said preparing myself to steal off on her.

"Get the fuck on trash. I just got my nails done." She waived her hand in my face, "Sca-daddle."

By this time we had an audience. I refused to walk away being punked. I threw a punch and before it could land every bit of four hundred pounds come crashing down on me.

* * *

Craving a blunt, I lit a Newport and tossed the cigarette lighter onto the nightstand—trying to forget today's events.

"Carly!" Synda called through the crack of my bedroom door.

"Synda, I'm not gone tell you again. I'm your mother!" I yelled back.

"Ma" She corrected herself. "I'm hungry and we ain't got nothin' to eat."

"It's some lunch meat in there."

"No it ain't. I ate the last piece of ham yesterday."

"I'm sure it's somethin' in there. Go round Ms. Vett's house and tell her you hungry. Take Mia over there too. I'm going to K&F later." It wasn't the first time I sent my kids to Vett's when I didn't feel like being bothered. Her house was like the safe haven for all the kids out here. If you were hungry, needed a place to sleep, needed your clothes washed or a baby sitter, you would go to her house. She was one of my main buyers. Every month she would buy two hundred dollars' worth of stamps. Now I was assed out. My mom's little three hundred was not going to feed five kids.

There was a knock on my door and then it opened. I picked up the pillow to hide my face. "Didn't I tell you to go to Ms.Vett's." I yelled.

The pillow was pulled from my face. It wasn't Synda, it was Beef, Ms. Vett's nephew from Rosegate. "Damn they fucked you up," he went to touch my purple eye and I moved.

"Fuck you Beef they jumped me."

"Yeah right," he laughed. "Check this out, me and my business partner got this new venture we 'bout to kick off...gone be major. In fact, we've been lookin' for someone like you to jumpstart it all," he said, handing me two fifties.

One hundred dollars? I took the money and tossed it on the nightstand next to the lighter.

"It can be very lucrative for you. That's if you're down."

I hope it pays more than a hundred fuckin' dollars. Regardless, I was always down whether it hurt, helped or ended up haunting me.

"I'mma call my peoples right now...we can get started tonight."

Asha

Chapter 4

Up three-hundred dollars with my rent and bill money already paid, this was enough to get my hair and nails done, I decided to call it quits for the night. I got dropped off at the BP and began walking home.

The trap boys were hanging out in their usual spot in front of the City Tavern or at K&F store rolling dice in between chasing cars and putting on mock rap battles. They were the same niggas that I saw last night when I walked by. *They ain't even been home to brush their teeth or wash their asses.* I kept a bottle of Listerine and a pack of baby wipes in my purse—not that either of the items could magically combat any sexually transmitted diseases. But to make myself feel better, I rinsed my mouth out and wiped my ass clean after each client; and took a bleach bath after a hard day's work. I didn't play that hitting it raw shit and was a regular at the Porter Center. Henrietta Johnson was too close to home. I didn't want the entire Bridge projects knowing my business.

A white minivan with a soccer-mom bumper sticker crept up the street. It stopped a few feet away from the liquor store. The driver was an anorexic brunette. *I bet none of her neighbors knows she's over here in the projects buyin' pills or dippers.* One of the trappers raced up to her driver's side window. They made their exchange and she went back to her middle class life in suburbia to get high. I just shook my head and kept walking.

The day had been profitable. I had serviced two tricks in the last hour. The worst of the two was a big, sweaty nigga that resembled WWE Star Mark Henry. It took all I had not to vomit on his ass. While serving him, I fantasized about Blair. His non-interest in my services and interest in getting to know me had intrigued me. I figured he was only in town for one night, making a drop and there was probably a one-in-a-million-lifetime chance that I'd ever see him again. *Oh, well.* I shrugged my shoulders.

At twenty-four, I had never had a boyfriend before—only repeat customers—and I had only been loved by one man, my father and maybe Cream. For a brief moment, I let my mind wonder to the possibility of one day running into Blair again, having a whirlwind romance and marrying him. But, I quickly returned to reality. I couldn't imagine any man trying to wife a prostitute—like the saying went, *you can't turn a hoe into a housewife.*

Starting to depress my damn self, I switched my thoughts to debating if I wanted Poetic braids or a bundle of Malaysian for a sew-in. I was getting excited about getting my hair done but what I most looked forward to was getting my hair washed and scalp massaged by Tink. She was the shampoo queen at Jael's—the salon where I got my hair done.

Just when I was about to make my mind up about the hairstyle I planned on rocking for the next two weeks, a car slowly approached behind me. I stuck my hand in my purse and palmed my stun gun.

"Ash-Kash, what's up ba-bay!"

I exhaled. It was Heedy, born Shaheed Miller.

"What's up, Heedy?"

"Nuthin'…just on the grind. You know how it is."

Heedy's cornrows hung past his shoulders. While other niggas had chopped their shit off, or wore dreads he stayed braided up. He was the color of a Reese's cup and had the prettiest, doe brown eyes like Allen Iverson. He was only sixteen and sold dope for a nigga named Manson aka Man-Man, who was running the game not only in South Bridge but all around the city. It was said that he was related to the Mason family but was shunned because of his reckless behavior. I knew Legend Mason, he was a big spender a few years back he tried to make me his young girl but I wasn't interested in a high profile relationship. He was too known and it would be bad for both of our businesses.

"I see you got that good paint job goin' on," I said, checking out his freshly painted lime green Starburst 89' Caprice sitting on 26" chrome rims with the Suicide doors. He was a part of the car club. That was a new thing. Motorcycle clubs for men and woman were played out. Everyone was on this tricked out car high. I attended a few car shows with Ki-Ki, my girl from Southbridge.

"You need a ride?"

"I'm straight."

"You sure? You know these niggas be up to no good out here…"

"I know. They were shootin' the other night in East Bridge they need to keep that shit over in South-had everybody dodgin' bullets. Thanks for lookin' out tho."

"No problem. Be safe out here, Babe."

I started to ask him if he knew a nigga in the game named Blair but decided against it. *Ain't no sense in thinkin' 'bout a nigga who ain't thinkin' 'bout me.*

I bent down to unbuckle my shoe straps. My feet were beginning to burn from standing on the corner all night long. Home was only a couple more blocks away and I was about to go the rest of the way barefoot. It was some trailer-park-trash shit to do, but I had forgotten my flip flops that I usually kept in my purse along with all the other stuff I had in there.

I bent over and looking through my legs, I saw flashing lights. *These motherfuckers get on my nerves.* It was the *jakes*. I wasn't a stranger to them and they weren't strangers to me. I had been locked up overnight on a few occasions but never charged. Thanks to Judge Massea.

"Stop and put your hands in the air," the officer demanded through the car's intercom.

"I am stopped. Can't you see I'm tryin' to unbuckle my damn shoes?" I yelled as I heard the police cruiser's doors open and close.

Two officers approached me, a young black cop who was nervous as hell and a middle-aged white cop. shining his flashlight all in my face.

"Can you not shine that light in my face?" I asked, cordially, trying to be nice.

"Shut the fuck up and spread'em," he said.

I hated these niggas but I knew I had to comply before I ended up like Sandra Bland. I didn't want to end up being a hash tag.

"What are you doin'?" I jerked my body back. He snatched me up by the neckline of my dress and pressed the barrel of his gun in between my thighs.

"Shut your mouth or my glock will be the next thing running up in ya."

Through the tears forming in my eyes, I looked him square in his face. He had arrested me before.

Officer Smith was his name. He removed the gun from under my dress and searched my purse.

He pulled out my stun gun.

"It ain't against the law to have a stun gun," I said, holding back my tears.

"It is tonight. So, unless you want to spend the night in a jail cell you're gonna have to do my partner a big favor."

"I'm cool," his partner said.

"Come on rookie…this is your initiation. This here gal is a Thomas; she and her dead auntie loves sucking dick. She has sucked plenty of dicks…"

"I'm good…really." The rookie said shaking his head.

Officer Smith looked at the Rookie with a threatening look. Reluctantly the rookie began to unbuckle his belt.

Nah, he's a bitch-ass nigga, I thought as the rookie cop slipped off his belted gun holster, unzipped and dropped his pants. What happened to Black Lives Matter? I wish I had my cellphone ready I would have streamed it live on Facebook. That would have stopped all this bullshit that was about to take place.

"Get on your knees."

"No." I tried to stand defiant.

"Get down or I will blow your brains out." Officer Smith pointed the gun towards my left temple. I dropped to my knees. I didn't want to be another hash tag.

Humiliated and fuming, I reached my unit. *What the hell?* Synda, Creams eight-year-old daughter was asleep in front of my house. I couldn't stand her mother, but she was an innocent child I wasn't going to take my dislike out on her. I scooped her up in my arms, took her into my house and laid her down on the couch. She tossed and turned but quickly drifted off back to sleep. *Where the fuck is Cream? Better yet, why the fuck ain't she home with her sorry ass mom?*

That Bitch tried to pop fly earlier and Big Zoe whooped up on her. She beat the brakes off that white bitch. Carly Felton, thought she was the project Kim K. She was thick for a white girl; hips and ass. And she had dyed and cut her long blonde hair to a jet black in order to appear more ethnic and often rocked a weave like every other chick in the hood. She had a cute face, blue eyes, a small nose and thin lips, which seemed to be fuller than I remember. We went to Kirk Middle School together. At the end of eighth grade she stopped coming to school-she got knocked up. I didn't see her for years until I caught her arguing with Shonni, my bougie neighbor across the street. Apparently she bumped her stroller into the chicks Infiniti -45. Shonni kept a fly whip and all types of delivery trucks in front of her crib. No one knew much about her except that she had three boys and her house looked like HGTV. I heard she gave it an extreme make-over. My girl Ki-Ki said she had granite counter top, stainless appliances and flat screens in every room. I don't know who she was fucking but whoever it was they were powerful as shit. It was a total violation to make changes to the units. I almost got put out for taking down the shades and adding blinds.

Still distraught over my ordeal with the jakes, I didn't even pay attention to the car parked on the side of the street directly in front of Shon's house at first. The way it was sitting there was suspect. I was praying it wasn't one of my crazed clients. Sometimes they would get out of hand and follow me home. I crept out my back door with my bat in my right hand and ran up on the car.

"Is it good to you, Daddy?" I heard a familiar voice.

"Hell yeah."

I swung the car door open.

"Oh, shit!" Cream shouted he continued to deep stroke her until he nutted. He turned around after catching his breath.

"You in here fuckin' while your daughter outside asleep. What kind of shit is that? I outta call DFS on your ass."

"Fuck you, Asha!"

40

Who the fuck is that? I pulled him up. Carly was laid across the back seat ass naked. "Wow, that's how we doin' it."

"Yo, Ash-wait!"

"Wait my ass-go get your daughter and go home with your white trash!"

"Bitch you the one whose trash, I don't sell my ass!" Carly said getting out the car.

"You need to do something bitch instead of depending on welfare all your life. Take care of your kids bitch, how about that!"

Back inside my unit, Cream had picked up his daughter. "I'm going to stop by tomorrow so we can talk,"

"Save your breath, your shit will be on the steps." I popped two blue xannies, went upstairs and started a bubble bath, pouring in a cup of bleach and some Epsom salt. I undressed and relaxed my body into the cold-like suds, closing my eyes and resting my head on the back of the tub. Soaking in bleach water could only wash away the night's external residue, leaving the internal dirt still trapped inside.

Shonni

Chapter 5

"Dale, what the hell did we discuss?" I said, swinging the door open.

"I know, but…"

"But what?" You cannot and I repeat you cannot be poppin' up at my crib like you payin' the bills up in here."

"I pay your car insurance and I just bought you that *Kors* purse that you wanted. Doesn't that count for something?" He asked, referring to the latest bag I had just added to my collection.

"Yes. It counts for the one fuck you get each month," I said, situating my hands on my hip. "I've got company on the way."

I lied to Dale about Nic being my cousin—mainly to protect Nic's reputation. He didn't question the relation. My mother was white and I took my looks from her. We could pass for twins, we both had honey blond hair, blue eyes and fair skin. The only black feature I possessed was my shapely figure. Now days most white girls even had that. I had kept it one hundred with Dale from day one. He was fully aware of my extracurricular activities with my other sponsors.

"Just let me taste it. That's all I want to do," Dale begged like a dope fiend ready and willing to sell his soul for another hit.

Dales thirst was a turn off. "Dale, go home to your wife. Watch a couple of pornos and imagine she's me."

"Let me pleasure you. It won't take but five minutes. Let me lick it," he teased, flicking his freakishly long tongue.

Shit. My thighs trembled as the words left his mouth and entered my ear. I was in trouble. Nic couldn't eat pussy to save his life but his dick was right to be white. I looked round to make sure no one was watching. Now since Manson and I was somewhat hood exclusive his goon squad and cousins had become the security team I hadn't asked for.

"Make this quick." I let Dale inside my unit.

He lifted my robe, removed my panties. He admired my bottom before guiding me to the couch.

"We gone have to do this on the floor," I said, in no hurry to christen my new sectional with cooch juice and saliva.

Dale gently laid me down on the living room floor and pried my legs apart. He didn't waste any time, sticking his head between my thighs and licking, sucking and eating me into ecstasy. *Damn. His tongue needs to bronzed and sat on a shelf.* As Dale wiped his mouth clean on the sleeve of his shirt, I heard Nic fumbling with the doorknob. When he realized it was locked, he banged on the door. I scrambled to my feet and rushed Dale down the hall and out the backdoor. *That was too close.*

* * *

Nic never spent the night. We exchanged pleasantries. He slept for an hour, showered after he woke, put the same clothes he arrived in back on and headed to his home—located behind a gated community in Greenville that he shared with his wife and small children. His routine suited me just fine; I never knew when Manson would be home anyway.

The night was still early, just a few minutes after midnight, when I walked him to the front door and pretended to enjoy his short and thick tongue dancing around in my mouth as we said our goodbyes.

I pulled myself away from him. "Don't forget...you promised me a new flat screen." I had asked Nic for a new television just as I was riding him into pleasure. He couldn't say no if he wanted to.

"I did?"

"Yes, you did."

"I'll have it delivered next week then," Nic promised.

I closed the door behind him, desperately in need of a drink and water wasn't the liquid that was going to quench my thirst. I needed a shot of Patron. I went upstairs and walked past my boy's empty room. I sighed deeply and closed the door. I decided to skip the Patron and go over to South Bridge to check on them. They were at Ms. Vett's house, which had become their home for the most part. They stayed with her five days out of the week. Half of the time when I would go to get them they didn't want to come. It hurt a little, but not enough for me to care. I made sure they were dressed fresh at all times. They had every game system, games, toys, sneakers and their own laptops. Welfare didn't pay for none of it. I was doing my job. I never had half of that stuff growing up. They should be grateful; majority of the kids out here would have loved to be in their shoes.

I threw on a cute tan linen jumper that I got from Ann Taylors and a red pair six inch Jimmy's. I grabbed my Michael Kors handbag and car keys. I knew it was close to one in the morning but you never know who you may run into and I refused to be caught slipping.

As I was walking to my car, I saw the guy Manson, referred to as Cream and his children's mom outside arguing. Their daughter was sitting in the middle of the street crying while they were carrying on. I shook my head as I listened in on the buffoonery. I was so happy that I didn't deal with these project clowns. Although Manson was from the streets, he wasn't in the streets. He let Heedy and the crews handle that. I drove down Heald Street and made a right on Townsend Place. I could have easily walked but I don't do the project thing. I pulled on the side of Ms. Vett's and was greeted by a slew of children running around throwing water on one another. *They bad asses need to be in the bed.* I remembered who their mothers were—young chicks with fucked up priorities. I suppose to those looking in from the outside, mine were also out of order as well.

I turned off my car and sat for a moment taking in my surroundings. There was a group of girls stag-gering around looking lost. They were outside of Brenda's place-the neighborhood trap house. Manson told me all about her. I thought he was joking until I saw her one day when we were dropping the boys at Ms. Vett's. She was small framed woman who looked like she was sixty and dressed like she was eighteen. She wore Cowtown designer shades and had one of her flunkies guiding her around. She was cussing out the lady across from Ms. Vett's; apparently she hadn't made good on paying her monthly tab. *How do you get drugs on credit?* I extended my head over the steering wheel to get a better look into the crowd before getting out. I heard they got loose over here. I usually ventured to these parts with Manson but he was out of town on business. They didn't look too much like a threat. I got out of the car and pushed the button to set the alarm. The girls' eyes watched as I strolled by with my head held high and nose in the air.

"Ain't that Man-Man's snow bunny." I heard one whisper. The one said, "She ain't white she wishes she was tho," I turned and looked at the brown skin girl. She stared at me with a grimacing look as she ate a bag of *Taki's*. She was jealous. They all were. This is the reason why I didn't deal with females to this day. I knocked on the door and the upstairs window opened.

"Hey cutie…you coming to pay daddy a visit," Kev said as he blew smoke from his Black out the window. His eyes were barely open, his wide grin showing a mouth full of teeth, were visible. He reminded me of that cat from Alice in Wonderland.

"Boy open the door before these creatures try to eat my face," I joked. He laughed and shut the window. I few seconds later I was greeted by Kev who had nothing on but a pair of boxers. I noticed his *man* was peeking out of the hole. I blushed and it enlarged like a shrinky-dink in an oven. "You see what you do to me babe. Why don't you come up stairs real quick so I can smack those cheeks," he grinned licking his lips. Kev had to be damn near every bit of forty. He was cool for the most part but he would never-ever smack nothing on me for free. I ignored his comments and walked up the steps and b-lined to the room where my boys slept. I crept the door open and peaked in. They were in the bunk beds that Manson had bought for them-knocked out. The Xbox One was connected to a thirty-six flat screen that was mounted on the wall. I turned the T.V and system off and went over and gave all three of them soft kisses on the cheek. I crept back out and shut the door. I turned around and was face to face with Kev and his monster dick was stabbing me in the abdomen. "Can I get a kiss?" he winked and directed his eyes to his penis. I pushed him out the way. "I at least need a two thousand dollar monthly allowance to look at that shit." I stated. He grinned, "Is that what Man-Man pays?" he asked.

"Don't worry about it-just know he handles all my needs financially and physically," I turned on my heels and headed to Ms. Vett's room. She was sitting on the side of her bed listening to WDAS. Evette Randall or Ms. Vett or Aunt Vett as everyone called her was the South Bridge Project Mom. She ran a licensed daycare twenty-four hours a day. Ms. Vett was in her early fifties. She was a big woman with a big heart for the people in her community. Manson introduced me to her a few months ago. He wanted to take me to Atlantic City and I tried to explain to him that I had nowhere for my kids to go. He asked why they couldn't go with their dad. I had never told anyone the identity of their father until that day. Manson felt some type of way about me having kids with the mayor. He said that answered a lot of his questions because he didn't understand how I was able to get away with defacing HUD property and not getting put out. I didn't call what I did defacing, I beautified the space. They should take notes. Like Dale, Manson believed Nic was my cousin. Manson didn't even know my father was black, he thought I was a blonde Italian. He had a thing for "white girls" It didn't matter if he thought I was Mexican as long as he took care of my needs I was good.

***

"Hey Ms. Vett. What's going on?" I took a seat on the dining room chair that was in her bedroom. She looked at the door like she was waiting for someone else to come in. She looked back at me, "Where's Man?" she asked.

"Out of town," I replied.

"What! Girl you came up here by yourself?" she laughed out loud, "Kev, Shonni done walked up here by herself ain't that crazy!" she was tickled to death.
"Her ass ain't walk nowhere, she drove that Infiniti up here so I can get up in that ass!" he laughed.

"Boy shut the fuck up, she ain't thinking about you. You better worry about who runnin' up in that raggedy bitch of yours ass," she shot at him. I couldn't help but snicker. Ms. Vett couldn't stand Kev's

49

girlfriend. I heard she was around my age and that was too young for his ass.

"Mom, you always got some smart shit to say!" he snapped no longer laughing.

"If you don't like it you can get the fuck out-honey!" she laughed and rolled her eyes.
The door slammed and that was the last I heard out of Kev that night.

"Ms. Vett you are a mess,"

"No I'm not, that raggedy ass girl he with is a mess," she leaned over towards me, "Girl, why did trifling ass Carly fuck Cream in the car while Synda was sleep *outside* in front of Asha's unit."

So that's what was going on...Ms. Vett knew everything that happened in both Bridges before it happened all the time.

"Oh! That's just sad. Why didn't they go to Carly's? Doesn't Cream stay there?"

Ms. Vett rolled her eyes, "Girl you know damn well Cream been playing house with Asha since Lynn died. Cream liked Asha since she came to the projects. She was a good girl and bad shit just kept happening to her."

"She can't be that great she prostitutes on the Ave." I said, like I really had room to be talking.

"Honey-I know you ain't talking," she rolled her eyes again.

"What?"

"What-my ass. You keep thinkin' people don't know what you do behind those doors. I know who those boys' dad is and I know your ass ain't related to the damn Masseas," she nodded her head with her plump lips twisted.

"What are you talking about?"

Anxiety was about to take over.

"Neil Santoki is the kids' dad, the mother fucker looks just like his beady-eyed ass. Nicolas saw his dads campaign add on the TV and kept calling him daddy, but I been knew. As for Dominic, honey all of my nephews use him whenever they are in trouble. I know his father and the whole Massea family well. Nic and his daddy love black pussy honey. We all know your ass is black. You ain't foolin' nobody with that Blonde hair and funny colored eyes. I got a cousin like you that can pass for white too."

"Ms. Vett does Manson know?"

"No. Not about Nic but he does know you are half black. You better cut it off with Nic before they both find out the truth. Man-Man has a temper and the Masseas...girl," she shook her head and gave me a look of pity. "We all have that *other side* that's not to pleasant for the naked eye," she added.

I had heard enough. I stood up, opened my bag and grabbed five one hundred dollar bills. I handed them to her, "Keep them for the summer so I can sort a few things out... please," she looked at the money and tucked it in her bra, "I'll make sure you have plenty of groceries and payment for keeping them. Manson…"

She cut me off, "Take of your business, they will be fine." She said.

Carly

Chapter 6

"I'm about to have company," I said to Synda before Beef showed up again when his so-called business partner, Pop, arrived. She was sitting Indian style on the living room floor, directly in front of the television.

"You always have company," she had responded without removing her eyes from the television screen.

Smart ass. I ignored her comment. "Scoot back before you fuck up your eyes."

She scooted back two inches. Shaking my head, I let her be. Leaving her alone in the living room without making sure she had ate dinner...I suppose I had done that a lot; left her alone.

I was aware of my faults and didn't appreciate Asha's outburst. Synda *was* a sleepwalker. It wasn't unusual for her to fall asleep in one spot and wake up in another. But, she had never wondered outside before. The thought of her getting struck by a car or even kidnapped numbed me. I recognized the fact that

I wasn't the best mother, but I loved my child regardless of what anyone thought—especially whore ass Asha, who I went way back with. At one point in our lives, we were cool. After I left school and had the kids we lost touch. It wasn't until last year that I found out the bitch my man was madly in love with was none other than Asha Thomas. She was my *opp* (enemy) since. She was a pretty thick chocolate girl with more curves than a coke bottle. She was book smart too. I heard she even had a job nursing before-why she started whoring who knows I guess it ran in her blood.

Pop had arrived with an iPad and two floor-model fluorescent lamps.

"What the fuck is all that for?"

"We film makers now," Pop said, heading straight to my bedroom with the equipment. "And we gone make you a super-fuckin'-star." Pop had a small head with protruding eyes henceforth his nickname. He was always animated-his features and behavior was a dead giveaway that he was a crack baby.

"I ain't wit' makin' no sex tape," I first told Beef, crossing my arms and standing defiant.

"Why not? Maybe Cream will want your ass again-he over there in East bridge fucking the shit out Asha's ass on a regular. He like freak bitches," Beef laughed.

"I don't know," I said, not believing that I was even actually thinking twice about doing this.

"Damn girl, I thought white girls took niggas away from black bitches not the other way around," Pop gave Beef dap as they clowned me.

Niggas always thought that because I was white that they could talk to me any kind of way. But, I wasn't the one. "Fuck you, Beef."

"Look, I'll blur your face out and nobody will ever know it's you. Once we get the website up and push it on the streets...they'll sell like candy. No, like perc thirties. It'll be a come up for us all."

"How much?"

"I'll burn like five hundred starting off and sell'em for ten dollars a pop. That's five-thousand dollars. We'll split it three ways. Then money should be streaming in from the site and we'll film some more scenes. We gone be good."

"Let's get this shit started," Pop said, placing a lamp on each side of my bed.   "Right now?"

"Yeah. We gotta get this paper."

I didn't even return to the living room to check on Synda. I just closed my bedroom door and let the show begin. I didn't think twice about Cream; he was probably over East Bridge fucking Asha like they said. *Lights, camera, action.*

First, Beef filmed me butt-ass naked on my knees sucking Pop's pencil dick. It was weird. Felt almost like I had a bone stabbing at the back of my throat. His shit taste like Irish Spring soap-at least it was clean.

He then instructed me to lay back on the bed, open my legs and then spread my pussy lips apart. He zoomed in with the camera. After getting the shot, he gestured for Pop to take the camera, he took a 40 ounce bottle and thrusted it as far as it could go in my pussy.

"This shit right here gone be better than that Mimi and Niko shit," Pop said. "Act like you want that shit," he directed. The truth was...I didn't want it or the life I was living anymore.

That's when, out of nowhere, Syncere barged into my bedroom like a bat out of hell.

"Mom, what the fuck!" he yelled and ran out.
We couldn't stop because I was in the middle of a shot.

* * *

"We done for the night," I asked.

"Yeah, it's a wrap," Beef said, packing up the equipment. "Damn, you a'ight?" He asked—not because of Syncere's presence but because I was coughing up a storm.

"Just...smoker's...cough," I said in between clearing my throat. My coughing spells had been getting worse over the years. *Gotta stop smokin'*, I thought, lighting another cigarette. It was a task, like changing your life around, that was easier said than done.

After Beef and Pop spilt I hopped out of the bed and slipped on some clothes. I had to talk too to talk to

Syncere about what he witnessed. He had been over my sister Nola's for over three months. He went about his business when I told him his real dad was none other Manson aka Man-Man. I wondered if he told Cream that he wasn't really his father. If so that would explain why he treated me the way he did.

I hadn't spoken to Man-Man, but I had seen him around—each time with that half-breed bitch on his arm who only wanted him for his money. It certainly wasn't for his looks. Man-Man looked like a big ass black gorilla. Without his throne as a street king, he would have probably been treated like a caged animal at the zoo. That goes to show the love I had for him. I loved him inside out.

Now, resentful, I blamed him too for the turn my life had taken. I went from being privileged to poor, living in the projects. As it turned out, Man-Man never loved me. He only wanted me for the moment. Man-Man and I met in Riverside. I had decided to run away from home for the night with my friend Nesha. I had experimented with weed, but she was a pothead from Brookmont and had been to Riverside to buy drugs numerous times.

She stopped at a corner where a group of young black boys were congregated. Man-Man approached the passenger side of the car. I stopped Nesha from rolling down the window.

"He's scary looking. What if he has a gun and tries to car jack us?"

"Carly, I know you ain't talking and you live in the projects," she said, rolling down the window.

"Sweetheart, I ain't got no reason to car jack y'all." He had heard me. "I got three BMW's."

My eyes were focused on his mouth. "Your teeth are sparkling."

"Yeah, it's called diamonds baby. What's your name?"

"Carly."

"Carly? I like that and I think I like you." He had my interest from then on and eventually...my heart.

"Why don't you ladies park your car and hang out with me and my boys for a while. Chill for a sec."

Nesha didn't hesitate putting her sixteenth birthday present in park—a red Accord. I was only thirteen but Nesha was my neighbor's niece and I got along well with her despite our age difference.

We followed Man-Man into a brick duplex. The inside was nicer than I had expected—no rats or roaches. A dated black leather couch and matching love seat were situated in living room. A chipped glass table rested between the distance of the couch and a bulky floor-model big screen. I noticed that the shade had a permanent bend from Man-Man and his boys peeking out the window every time a car passed by or there was a knock at the door—paranoia was a known side effect of trapping.

Niggas were in and out of the duplex, dropping off crumbled five, ten and twenty dollar bills to Man-Man and picking up more products to sell—consumer demand was high.

Man-Man sat in the middle of the couch, between Nesha and me. He emptied a plastic bag full of weed onto the coffee table, removed stems, hollowed out the center of a Garcia and rolled the fattest blunt I had ever seen. Nesha caught the eyes of a nigga named Dollar and the four of us smoked ourselves unconscious. At the end of the night, I could barely remember my name. The next morning, I woke up undressed on a mattress in one of the two bedrooms. I was so wrapped up in that nigga that I didn't think twice about my boyfriend in South Bridge.

* * *

"Let me in. I need to speak to Man-Man," I told Dollar.

"Hold on," he said. "Man-Man, Carly here....says she needs to talk to you," he spoke into the walkie-talkie in his gigantic hand.

"What the fuck she want?"

"Nigga, I don't know. She yo' bitch."

"Just ask her."

"He said what you want."

Like an escaped mental patient, I started screaming and shouting—making a scene in front of Man-Man's trap house.

"Man, this hoe is crazy. If she don't shut the fuck up I'mma smack her white ass!"

"Shit! Let her ass in."

I couldn't distinguish Man-Man's trap house from a strip club. Smoke, liquor and ass were all in the air. A few of his foot soldiers were scattered round-a-about, receiving lap dances from big-booty broads making their ass cheeks clap to the beat of the music that was blaring from the large speakers located throughout the place. Others were counting money, weighing out powder or bagging weed. I waved to Heedy who was every bit of eleven at that time.

"What's up, Carly. I heard you was outside wild'n out."

"That nigga wasn't gone let me in to see Man-Man."

He was sitting behind a large mahogany desk buried in stacks of cash and coke. My intentions weren't to try and reconcile our relationship but to strictly to ask for some money. *He owes me.* However, my emotions got the best of me and my eyes begin to water.

"What did I do to make you stop wantin' me?" I cried. I cut my eyes at the young girl stretched out on the black leather couch in the corner of Man-Man's office.

"Man-Man, you better get her white ass before I do."

"Get me? Bitch, Bye."

"Fuck you Sleazy Sue." She stood up.

"Both y'all need to shut the fuck up." He said, darting his eyes at me. "Carly, I know you didn't come down here to start some bullshit. What...you want some money?" He laughed. "Ask that nigga Cream-Oh I mean Syncere daddy for some money. Oh yeah-I forgot he mines...you just named him after another nigga"

"Don't be like that-you said you didn't want nothing to do with the baby so I had no choice but to put it on Cream."

"Bitch get your young dumb ass outta here before your face ends up on a milk carton," he was cruel. I couldn't believe this was the man I fell in love with.

I turned and walked away. With one foot out the door, someone grabbed me by my arm. I turned around defeated. It was Heedy.

"Here." He tucked a hundred dollar bill in my hand. "Maybe it will help."

Asha

Chapter 7

I got out of bed and headed to the bathroom, clicking on the light. *Damn!* I scared myself. I was looking a hot-ass-early-morning-hood-mess and my quick weave was looking like who-did-it-and-what-for—dry, tangled and full of lint balls. I sprayed some oil sheen on it, brushed it out and quickly tied a scarf over my head. I walked out the bathroom and I heard my front door open.

"Who that?" I yelled.

"It's me Cream-Asha we need to talk,"

"Ain't shit to talk about go on back to your snow girl and them kids. I ain't got time for the drama-for real."

I stepped back in the bathroom and turned on the shower. I had to make sure I was fresh for my salon appointment. I slipped the strap to my nightie off my shoulders and stepped out of it. I opened the shower curtain before I stepped in and felt a tug at my waist and wetness against my ass cheeks. *Here this dude* go… "Cream I said get the fuck on-I'm not fucking you no more," I tried to pull away but his hold was tight with his free hand he spread one of my ass cheeks and plunged his tongued deep inside my dook shoot. My body quivered on contact. I bent over the sink as he slithered his tongue in and out of my hole causing my twat to spasm. *Damn*…he knew my weakness and I hated him for it. I played with my clit while he tossed my salad as my mind went back to Blair. I closed my eyes and pretended it was him giving me pleasure. I moaned out loud and whispered, "Fuck me." Cream wasted no time throwing on a condom and sticking his fat seven inches in my juice box. The sloshing of his dick submerged in my oils was like music to my ears.

"Fuck me harder," I yelled. Cream pushed in as deep as he could go and sped up his rhythm. I slammed my ass back hard each time causing him to grunt and moan. I was about to explode. "I'm cumming Blair!" I shouted to the high heavens. The movement stopped and my eyes opened. That's when I knew I had fucked up.

"Who the fuck is Blair?"

Cream's limp dick fell from my box. I turned around slowly. The look on his face was one I had never saw before. It was between crazed and hurt.

"That was your last piece of pussy from me I hope you enjoyed it," I said, avoiding the argument he wanted to have. I got in the shower and started washing up and singing Darling Nikki by Prince. I peeked out the curtain and he was gone. I laughed to myself. I couldn't believe that I yelled out ol' boy's name like that. I knew Cream's feelings were crushed but he was going to have to get over it. I went to step out and was met with a swift right to the side of my head. "What the fuck…" I yelled.

Cream was hovered over top of me throwing blows wherever he could land them. "You two bitches think you can play with me, I'mma show y'all hoe's that I ain't to be fucked with!"

He was going off like a wild man. I screamed for help as I fought back. I was wet so he couldn't get a hold of me like he wanted to. I managed to get out of the small bathroom I ran towards the stairs he grabbed at my hair and snatched off the scarf. I held the rail as I kicked at him. He continued yelling calling me and Carly all types of names. I went to kick him away and lost my footing. I tumbled down the stairs hitting my head on the front door. Cream took advantage of the situation and grabbed me by the neck. He slapped me until I could taste blood in my mouth. I had tricked with all types of men and I never-ever ended in a situation this brutal.

"You dirty bitches think ya'll can play me. Both of y'all was in on it from the beginning. I can't believe that I didn't see it coming." He cried. I had no idea what this dude was talking about. "I'mma treat you like you like to be treated-like a Hoe!" He pulled his dick out and shoved it down my throat. I began to gag and shake violently. He grabbed my head and pinned it against the door with his pelvis and pushed himself deeper in my mouth. Vomit was lounged in my airway. "Suck this dick bitch!" I kicked my legs fighting for air. I couldn't go out like this. Using the little strength I had left I bit down hard on his dick. Cream hollered to the top of his lungs and rolled off of me. Tears streamed down my face as chunks of vomit and thick saliva spewed from my mouth. I tried to get to my feet and catch my breath. I could barely see straight. I managed to get my door open and crawled outside stark naked. I used the gate to pull myself up. I heard Cream yelling my name and moving around. I knew I had to get away. I looked behind me and I saw him come out the screen door holding his groin.

"I'mma kill you bitch!" I started to run but was stopped by another hit to the face. This bitch Carly started wind milling on me. This shit was too damn much for me. By now a crowd had formed and people from both sides of the projects were watching. I swung back. I was weak as shit but I refused to let a white bitch beat me down in the hood. We rolled off the grass into the street.

"Whoop that trick!" Somebody blurted out. Hell, I didn't know if they were cheering for or against me. I felt my body being lifted by my hair and Cream put me in a headlock while Carly wailed on me.

"Oh shit they banking her!" Someone else yelled.

"World Star!" someone else sang.

"They continued to team me. Until two shots from a glock caused them to stop.

Not knowing where the shots were coming from people started to run. I lay in the street naked beat down. Carly stood there like she saw a ghost. Cream backed away mumbling. I saw someone walking towards me and covered me with a blanket helping me to my feet.

* * *

I entered Shonni's immaculate unit. She took me to her bathroom and handed me a rag and towel. "Clean yourself up...I'll bring you something to wear in a minute."

"Here," she handed me a clean set of clothes. The metallic bronze toned mosaic tile on the floor heated the bottom of my feet. Her entire unit looked as if belonged on MTV cribs. I got in the shower to wash away blood and vomit. I cleaned it out and ran bath water in the jetted tub. I tried to wrap my mind around what happened. I was mad at myself for leading Cream on as long as I did. I thought about my life and everything that happened since I was introduced to the other side of my family. What did I do to deserve this? I snorted. That was a rhetorical question, I was a Hoe.

God frowned upon jezebels. I lay back in her jetted tub and tried to calm my body. *Boom-Boom...Boom!* My body trembled and I busted out in tears. I hated being out here. Where was my guardian angel? I looked up to the heavens, "God I promise I will leave this shit alone if you offer me a way out!" I pleaded. I prayed that he too hadn't turned his back on me.

Shonni

Chapter 8

I watched out the window as the CSI van combed through the area with yellow crime scene tape. Manson had sent Cream to an early grave. Word has it he had stolen a package from one of Heedy's trap houses. It just so happen that Manson was at my house when he wanted to go Ike on my neighbor. Manson took the opportunity to confront him. He shot the gun to clear the area and told me to bring the girl in the house. What got me was the look on the white broads face when she saw Manson. I thought she was about to shit herself. He starred at her and she ran off. I guess Cream didn't say what Manson wanted to hear. Three shots and his ass was laid out gurgling and choking off his own blood. That wasn't the first time I saw someone get murked. I was from West Baltimore that shit happened all the time. Manson told me to get Asha dressed and for us to roll out for the day. I happily did as I was told. Normally I would go solo, but this time I had a companion to roll with. The circumstances were fucked up, but I was going to try to make the most of it. It took a total of four trips out to my car and back to carry in all of the shopping bags we had accumulated during one trip to the mall. I wasn't sure if my shopping addiction had originated out of the circumstances of never having shit as a child or out of pure greed; probably a little bit of both. Either or, there was no denying it, I had a serious problem.

I had so much stuff that I didn't have to wear an outfit twice—ever. I shopped like I had money to blow—never worrying about running out of cash because to me, money didn't grow on trees; it hung from a nigga's nut sacks and as long as there were wealthy niggas to be fucked, there was always money to be made. But sometimes, a chick needed to be selective. The three grand that Heedy had offered to me on the low to "entertain" Manson's Haitian connect was enticing, but I was leery of getting involved. I think it was a set up. They knew damn well I was with Manson. Going against him could be deadly. With that, I passed on Heedy's offer.

After a long hot shower, I moisturized my body with my favorite *Bath & Body Works* scented lotion, Warm Vanilla and then removed the plastic cap and scarf from over my head. I watched the curls from my roller wrap bounce back into place. Earlier, I took Asha to her hair appointment at Jael's. After her beat down I thought that was the last place she wanted to show her face. She said she was good and I wasn't about to argue. It's not like she had black eyes or anything, she looked alright. I was hesitant about letting another stylist besides Krist do my hair, but it turned out better than I had anticipated. Having flawless skin, I didn't need to wear much makeup. I put on some mascara, lightly brushed some plum blush on my cheeks and drowned my lips in clear MAC lip gloss. I dabbed some perfume—between my thighs, behind my kneecaps, ears and on my neck and chest. And then I slipped into a little—and I do mean little— black dress. There was a party at Lavish and Manson wanted me to be there. It's not like Nic, Neil, or Dale for that matter would be there. I asked Asha if she wanted to go. She declined. Against my better judgment I told her to chill at my house until I got back. Manson didn't want her home in case the detectives had caught wind of the fight that had taken place before Cream was murdered. He knew she was still rattled and didn't want her talking too much.

I went into my self-made, walk-in closet and picked out a pair of black stilettos, fitted my feet in them and grabbed a matching black, Gucci clutch, stopping to admire my reflection in the large, chrome G that fastened it shut. *My lip gloss is right'*. I thought to myself before walking out the door.

Heading over to my car, my eyes traveled across the street—noticing the cops talking to Carly. I made a mental note, started my car and pulled off.

I was stopped at the light by K&F when I saw Dream eating a bag of chips, her sister Ki-Ki was by her side as usual. They were Manson's cousins, the only females that I talked to in the projects

. Shonni!" I heard Ki-Ki calling my name and walking towards me.

"Hey, Ki-Ki."

"You goin' to Lavish?"

"You know it."

"Me, too. Can I get a ride?"

"Yeah. Hop in."

Just as Ki-Ki was about to open the back door to my car, Dream, her seven-month pregnant sister came wobbling up to the car.

"Ki-Ki, where you goin'?"

"I'll be back in five minutes."

"Bitch, why you lyin'?" she snapped.

"Girl you been having pains all day and I thought you was cooking some steak and rice."

I shook my head. I did not have time for sibling conflicts, watching them go at it made me think about my very own siblings. I hadn't talked them since Neil made me call my mother to let her know I was fine. To my surprised she wasn't too happy to hear from me. She told me I was going to hell for stealing from them and I would have no good fortune for abandoning my family. *If only she could see me now.* She would have no choice but to eat her words.

Dream rolled her eyes and walked away from the car eating her bag of chips.

"Somebody lookin' for Asha..." she said.

"Who, the police?" I asked.

"Naw some sharp ass big nigga,"

"Maybe it was one of her clients," I shrugged my shoulders.

"Probably, but what I want to know is why is Dosha walkin' this way in that too little ass dress?"

Dosha lived three units down from Ki-Ki. She was surviving off of her deceased mother's benefits— forging her name and cashing her social security check every month. *Her ass is goin' straight to jail when the law catches on.* She was a big girl, didn't have two inches of hair to braid and her gums were black as shit. But, as long as she had a carton of Newports and a bottle of Teleport, she was content as a vampire in a pool of blood.

"Dosha, where the hell you goin' lookin' like Precious?"

"Fuck you, Ki-Ki. I know I look good. I don't care what you say," Dosha said, adjusting her cleavage and opening the back door.

I turned to Ki-Ki, and gave her the-*what the fuck* look. I didn't know this big bitch and I was stunned

72

that she had the audacity to open up my car door. Ki-Ki laughed. I didn't see shit funny.

"Yo Dosha, you can't be opening my people's car like that." Ki-Ki laughed.

"Oh my bad," her breathing sounding as if she had a whistle lounged in her lungs, "I thought y'all was waiting for me."

"Bitch how the fuck you figure that?" Ki-Ki said.

"You want me to get out?"

"No it's fine," I said. She had already stuffed her big ass in here. I put the car in gear so we could head to the spot. Just as I was about to pull off Carly came darting out the cut wearing a sheer black cat suit, exposing her black bra and boy shorts and a pile of make-up over her battered face. Asha *fucked her shit up.*

"Who the hell do she think she is…Nicki Minaj?"

"Ki-Ki, you're a nut," I said, laughing.

"Did she ever find out who Syncere's father was?" Dosha asked.

"I thought her kids were by Cream," I replied, puzzled.

"No. Cream got a test done on the low after lil Syncere hipped him to some shit. Those other two are his but lil Syn not," she informed me.

"Wow" I said.

"Damn!" Ki-Ki sparked a blunt; the weed had to be exotic that shit stank so good. I normally didn't smoke, and I normally didn't hang with bitches or let prostitutes hang in my house. I figured I might as well enjoy today. Who knows what tomorrow would bring.

* * *

The caliber of men I associated with rarely crossed the thresholds of Lavish—not to take anything away from the street-collar niggas who were in and out of the hot ass club throughout the night, taking breaks from chasing that paper. Their pockets were deep, but I was satisfied with my married-white-collar sponsors and not interested in adding a dope boy to my team. I already had the main supplier why fuck with the help. Ki-Ki, Dosha and I went straight to the door walking past all those who stood in the long line. The place was nice to be in Delaware. Nothing like the spots in Atlanta, Miami or Vegas. The décor was posh —white leather sofas sat up against the walls. In another room were pool tables and more places to sit. Still, Lavish was the hot spot for the young and the old in the hood who wanted to show boat. It wasn't unusual to see the young grandmother-mother-daughter and father-son duos in the club partying right alongside each other to the break of dawn—the parent couldn't be distinguished from the child.

We pushed our way through the growing crowd to the bar. I had a four-drink limit—enough alcohol to give me a buzz but not enough to completely impair my senses. In the privacy of my own home, it was another story. I drunk until my head spun.

While Ki-Ki, and Dosha ordered their drinks, I stood at the end of the bar waiting for the nigga I was batting my eyes at to send me over a drink. From the faded polo that he had on and the dirt and oil under his nails, it was evident that he wasn't a baller but a blue-collar brother. *He'll be good for one drink.* Seconds later, a shot of Henny was placed in front of me.

My drink benefactor gestured for me to join him. I declined, mouthing to him a thank you and giving him a good look at my plump bottom as I turned and walked away. He became a memory of my past and I became a predator on the hunt for another nigga to by me another drink.

Ki-Ki and Dosha swiped a table from a couple of females who had temporary left to empty their bladders. "You beat," Ki-Ki said, taking a seat. Dosha sat down at the table across from her and immediately slid her un-pedicured feet out of her heels.

"Dosha, you need to put your shoes back on. We tryin' to attract niggas…not scare them away," Ki-Ki laughed.

"Niggas don't give a fuck about a bitch's feet if what's between her legs stays tight and wet."

"Well, we know you loose and dry. So, put your hooves back in your shoes."

"Y'all two stay at each other."

"She just jealous," Dosha said.

"I ain't even gone respond to that unbelievable shit you just said." Ki-Ki downed her drink.

"Where the hell did Carly go?" I asked, scanning the club.

"Better check the men's restroom," Ki-Ki said, hi-fiving Dosha. "You know how she do."

They said Carly was known to disappear and reappear with her hair out of place and cum stains on her clothes. Apparently, she was some sort of amateur porn star. They said her DVD's were a hit in all three city projects.

I decided to go look for Manson, it was getting crowded and this was not my crowd-at all. The nigga in the faded polo found me and grabbed my arm. He was actually handsome. His shape-up was on point and he was taller than he appeared sitting down on the barstool. I looked him over and was immediately disappointed—not that he ever had a chance of making my team. His tan Timbs were dirty and the knees of his jeans were stained. *He's a bum ass nigga.*

"Hey, ma. What's good?"

"Oh, hey! Thanks for the drink," I said, attempting to be nice.

"Is that all I get?"

This nigga act like he took me to Barney's and dropped ten stacks... "Nigga, you didn't do shit but buy me a ten-dollar drink."

"Nigga?" He shook his head. "I know your white ass ain't..."

"Wrong I'm not White-I'm bi-racial and if you knew who I was connected to-you would watch your mouth." I rolled my eyes and left him standing where he was but not before hearing him whisper something under his breath.

"What was that?"

"I said...don't let your eyes fool you."

"Nigga...please."

Carly

Chapter 9

After my failed attempt at killing myself back in the eighth grade, when I found out I was pregnant, my social worker sent me to a shrink. *That's white people for you.* To say the least, the sessions weren't helpful. But, they had sparked my interest in human behavior and before meeting Man-Man—when I was on track to attend my uncles' alma mater, the University of Delaware—I had decided that I wanted to major in psychology. Now more than ever, my own behavior fascinated me; why I continued to choose wrong when I knew what was right. Why did anybody?

What I concluded was three-parts. While I had the desire to change my ways and create a better life for myself and my kids; mouths still had to be fed and bills still had to be paid; old habits didn't die overnight and sometimes it all boiled down to the company we kept. *Birds of a feather flocked together.*

* * *

"You got knocked the fuck out!" Dream said, staring at my bruised face.

"What-the-fuck-ever. I'm still standin' ain't I?"

"You gone need some clown make-up to cover that shit up," she continued. "Better yet...some spray paint." She laughed. "You know I saw that DVD, Umm-hmm."

"What you umm-hmm'n about? We all spread our legs the same."

"Some of us more than others," she remarked, walking out the door. *She's got her nerves.*

I sat down on my couch feeling lonely as shit. I couldn't believe that my children's father was gone and I went to Lavish to fuck and suck my pain away. The detective had hemmed me up when I went to put candles and a bear at his memorial spot. He asked me a bunch of questions I was too fucked up to answer them, besides I had no rap for them. I couldn't allow myself to get caught talking to the police. This was the streets and you had to live by the code or get dealt with. Syncere heard what happened to the father he had known and ran off. Ms. Nett had Synda and Symia. The picture of Man-Man bustin' his gun played over and over in my head; I was so mad at myself for not doing anything. There wasn't shit I could do he would have killed me too. What really had me fucked up was none of his so called boys did anything, soon as they saw man they disappeared. Now they were all partying with R.I.P T-shirts like they really gave a fuck. I told Cream not to fuck wit Manson but he wanted to try and prove a point. Then there was Asha. He couldn't leave her as alone. If he wasn't over there he would be here right now.

* * *

It was every bit of 1am and I couldn't sleep. I decided to go the Grey House to see what was poppin' off. I had $225 to my name—$50 from Beef, the $100 that Kev gave and $75 from some random nigga at the club… It was all to help with the funeral. I could spare twenty dollars for a couple of drinks.

"Hey, honey." Spirit hopped off of the bar stool and wrapped her arms around me. She also lived in East Bridge and had ten kids—five boys and five girls. With ten kids, I know she brought in bank, collecting a hefty income tax check every year; she did have an entire cheerleading squad and football team to feed.

"I like that outfit," she said, looking me up and down. "Where did you get it? I'm gone get me one."

"Please don't," Dream said. "The human eye can only take so much."

"Why you always got somethin' to say?" she asked Dream.

"Why you got so many damn kids?" Dream retorted.

"Why you about to drop a load and at the bar..." she wrinkled her nose, "You act like you ain't got more than one kid."

"Bitch, this is my third and they have the same dad can you say that...."

Silence.

"Oh-that's what I thought,"

"Don't be all up in mine's," Spirit shot back.

"All I was tryin' to say was that you know your ass is too damn big to wear that outfit Carly got on. Shit, she shouldn't even be wearin' it," Dream looked at us both. She was right—about Spirit; not me. With ass on top of more ass, Spirit would be banned from going out in public in a sheer bodysuit. Along with her voluptuous frame, she was dark skin and wore her hair buzzed blonde like Kanye's old jump off, Amber Rose.

"What's up girl?" I asked her.

"'Bout to beat a bitch's ass."

Here we go. Spirit was that bitch in the hood who thought every other bitch was after her man, which puzzled me. *Who the fuck wants a nigga who is taking care of ten kids, that ain't his?*

"Why? What happened?"

"Some bitch tryin' to get all up on Tim. I had to get me a drink first...before I whoop her ass."

"She better watch out," I said. "Cause everybody know you don't play when it comes to Tim."

"Yup, just like you didn't play about Symai. Girl, I hope they get whoever did it," Spirit glared over in the direction of Teena.

"Ain't Teena your cousin?" I asked, just to make sure I wasn't making shit up.

"Yeah, skinny bitch can't find a man of her own."

"Well, more power to y'all. I'm about to get my groove on." Just like a white girl, I headed to the dance floor to dance by my damn self. I couldn't even find my rhythm good before being interrupted.

"Carly!"

Who in the hell?

Beef and his business partner-sidekick Pop were in the club. *I can't get rid of these niggas to save my life.* Beef had a hand full of DVD's in his hand.

"I told you these babies would sell like crack. You alright tho?"

"Let me see." I ignored his latter statement, he fucked with Manson heavy. He already knew I was fucked up. He handed me one of the DVD's. "What the fuck?" The title of the flick was *Carly's Getting her Pink Cheeks Beat*. "Why the hell you put my real name out there?"

"Calm that shit down. That name is basic as fuck, everybody knows a Carly."

"Niggas ain't dumb. I'm sure if my eight-year-old daughter can put two and two together...anybody can.

"What can I say? It is what it is. Look, we got the camcorder in the car. I was thinkin' we could shoot another scene in the bathroom. It'll be real hot."

"Fuck that. I ain't doin' another scene until I get my money from the scenes we already done shot."

My life literally flashed in front of me. Before I could say another word, Pop had a glock pressed against my temple. *This nigga is bipolar.* He had gone from zero to a hundred in two seconds.

"You gone do the fuckin' scene or I'm gonna bust ya head and then find that cute little daughter of yours and do the same to her, ya'll be seeing that dead nigga Cream sooner than you expected. Don't play me. You said you was down and I done invested my time and money in you."

He eased the gun away from my head. I caught my breath. "Come the fuck on. I ain't got all night."

We headed to the men's restroom.

Asha

Chapter 10

Jael had hooked me up. My bob was fly enough to be showcased in a Bronner Brothers hair show but with beauty came pain. My damn scalp was hurting like hell. He had braided my hair so tight that my eyes were slightly slanted. I wasn't sure if the pain was from the braids or the fight. *Damn, my head is aching'.* I felt a migraine coming on.

Digging deep into the bottom of my bag amongst all the shit I had in it, I finally felt the bottle of percs I was searching for. I swallowed two pills—dry. Being my own boss, there was no one but myself preventing me from calling it a night and heading home. And the more I thought about my entire situation, I was beginning to realize that I was the only obstacle standing in the way of a better life for myself—But, creating a new life for myself was easier said than done. *Two more,* I said to myself. *Two more tricks and I'm done for good.* After paying bills, getting my hair done and shopping with the Shonni chick, I was broke and in need of some cash which always seemed to be the case. I knew I had promised God I would stop. I had to get the other day's events out of my mind.

Cream had violated me in the worst way but I didn't wish death upon him. He had children. I tried not to think about it. I got dressed and went out Shonni's back door. She was on her couch smashed.

Business on the Ave. had slowed down and while waiting for the next trick to roll up, I found myself standing on the corner reminiscing about my encounter with Blair—wishing that I was his Cinderella and he was my prince. Just as I was imagining myself adorned in a custom made Vera Wang wedding dress that accentuated my twenty-four-inch waist and entangled in a waltz with a tuxedo-clad Blair, my fairytale fantasy was rudely interrupted by commotion on the other end of the boulevard.

"Bitch, where the rest of my money?"

"That's all of it. I promise. Please...please don't hit me." Janelli barricaded her face behind her arms, anticipating the worst.

"Bitch, you been gone trickin' for two hours and you hand me sixty-three dollars. You must think a nigga can't count."

Janelli was a Mexican chick that whored for a pimp named Tuffy. Janelli had immigrated to the United States from Mexico in hopes of securing a better future for her and her family. Unfortunately, she crossed paths with Tuffy and he sold her a dream only to turn her life into a nightmare. Thinking she was joining another cleaning company with higher pay, she had quit her job with Merry Maids to join Tuffy's roster of working girls. She had accepted the position without fully comprehending the job description of "working girl." Now, she understood and spoke English just as fluent as she turned tricks.

Janelli was down on her knees pleading with Tuffy not to beat her ass. *That's the reason I work for my damn self.* Tuffy—thought he was still in Chi-town lookin like a buff Samuel L. Jackson. He tried to come at me after Auntie Lynn was killed.

"When you gone let Big Tuff rescue you?" He had approached me on the Ave. one night. "Come be a part of my team. I'll make you a starter. You can get all the playin' time you want."

I stared his short ass down. "If you were the last nigga on earth with a life jacket and I was drownin' I still wouldn't take that shit. So, fuck you."

"It's an open invitation, baby. When you're ready, just let a pimp know."

When I turned his invite down, the little nigga foolishly had the nerve to threaten me.

"This Ave belongs to me. I've just been bein' nice to you…lettin' you turn tricks in my territory for free but that shit's about to change."

"Fuck outta here, only nigga that own Cash Ave. is Lee Mudd and my family got a pass to do as we please so get da fuck on with that lame shit!" I told his Joe ass. "You don't run shit, especially not New Castle Avenue. As much pussy as my Aunties and cousins sold here- Get the fuck out of my face." And that was the end of the discussion. He never threatened me again.

Tuffy punched Janelli in the gut. *Damn.* She belted over in pain and cried. I felt sorry for her but on the corner, it was every broad for herself and I wasn't about to come between a pimp and his hoe. He then grabbed her by her ponytail and stuffed her into the back of the canary yellow and pink Lincoln he was driving before going to hassle the other girls he had working the night shift.

My thoughts returned to Blair. Every car that turned down the Ave, I had hoped it was a Range. Not just any Range Rover, but the one he was driving with him in it. I closed my eyes and crossed my fingers. All of the hope that I had quickly dissipated as the white minivan stopped in front of me. I recognized the vehicle immediately. *She got the wrong corner or got me fucked up.* I didn't sell pills; I sold pussy. And unlike the other working girls, I did discriminate. I serviced men and men only. No women or anything in between. *Her ass is probably pilled- up* I approached the minivan, thinking that I was going to see the strung out soccer mom who I had witnessed copping from one of the trap boys that night in front of K&F store. Instead, it was a middle-aged white man. Her husband, I guessed. *Life in the suburbs must be fucked up.* Despite the lingering wrinkles under his eyes, he wasn't bad looking. In fact, his salt-and-pepper hair made him sexy in an old school Richard Greer kind of way. He was far more attractive than the ghouls I had slobbed off a few days ago.

"How may I help you?" I asked, sounding like I was selling hamburgers and French fries instead of an ass-and-tits combo.

"How much?"

"Depends on what you want. I charge two hundred for a straight sex and an additional fifty if you want to include a blow job."

"Okay. Where?"

"We can pull into a dead in and do it in the back of this minivan for all I care. Just as long as I get my money up front."

"Okay."

He was mild mannered and had a cool demeanor. *This might not be so bad.* I jumped in the minivan and guided him down the nearest cut by Eden Park. He put the van in park and turned off the ignition. We stared at each other. It was obvious that this was his first time picking up a prostitute.

"Did you decide what you want?" I asked.

"Just intercourse. No blow job."

Straight and to the point. Good. I did not feel like suckin' another dick tonight. "That's going to be two hundred dollars."

He reached for his wallet and pulled out two crisp hundred-dollar bills. "Come on," I crawled into the backseat of the van and he followed.

"Should I take my clothes off?" He asked.

"Nah, just pull down your pants," I instructed him as I lifted up my dress.

"Here, put this on." I handed him a condom.

He did as I asked and I climbed on top of him. He moaned and palmed my waist as I slid down on his dick. "Oh...my...never...felt anything...so good."

I sat in his lap, rocking back and forth. "Is it good to you, sweetie?" I added in some excitement to his experience since he was a first timer.

"Yes...yes...yes!" He came in under two minutes, trying to rest his head on my chest. But I quickly got up, pulled my dress back down and crawled back into the front seat of the minivan.

"When can I see you again?" He asked me like we had been on a date or something.

"Look, as long as you got the money, I got the time," I said, stepping out of the van. "You know where to find me."

"I'm John by the way," he said.

I waved goodbye, keeping my anonymity.

"Thanks," he yelled out.

* * *

BOOM! BOOM! BOOM! The rattling of the trunk of the black-on-black, 1985 refurbished Monte Carlo turning onto the avenue, could not be ignored. I was the only girl on the corner. The others were either with tricks or with Tuffy. I stood back, hoping the car would keep it moving, but it stopped right in front of me. The passenger side window was already rolled down and I could smell remnants of marijuana smoke.

"Asha."

Fuck. I didn't move.

"Asha, bring your fine ass over here."

I walked to the car—like I was walking to my death. "What the fuck you want?" I asked Dameon.

"Who the fuck you talkin' to?" He asked. "Get the fuck in. I'm a payin' customer."

"Look…one of Tuffy's girls should be back on the scene in a few. Roll back through in about ten minutes," I said, trying to talk him into fucking another hoe. Tink and I weren't BFF's, but I considered her a friend.

"I don't want any of those other hoes. I want you tonight."

"I just can't do it," I said. "You know Tink, my peoples."

He reached into the open duffle bag next to him in the front seat and tossed a stack onto the passenger side seat. "It's yours if you want it."

I didn't want it. I needed it. I hesitated. Like church folk believed that there was power in prayer, those of us in the streets knew the power of the almighty dollar.

"Where we goin'?" I asked him as we passed the Budget where I thought we were headed instead we hit the highway.

"I gotta make a quick stop."

"Nigga you drawin'! I ain't tryin' to get caught up in no shit. Just drop me off at the room."

"Just chill. It'll be quick."

We pulled up in front of the back door of what once was a daycare but was now Man-Man's trap house in Browntown. He scooped up the duffle bag full of cash and approached Dollar, who stood guard at the steel door Man-Man had gotten installed when he took over the place. Dollar let Dameon through and he disappeared inside. Minutes later, the door opened and Dameon walked out. But, he wasn't alone. Man-Man was behind him and behind Man-Man was Jella—the new stylist at Jael's. *He fuckin' her now?* I ducked as soon as I spotted her, praying that she hadn't caught a glimpse of me in the front seat of Dameon's car.

The driver side door flung open and Dameon hopped in. I was ducked down low in the passenger side seat.

"Why the fuck you duckin'? I ain't hear no gun shots 'round this motherfucker."

"That chick Man-Man was with, Jella. You know she work for Tink. I think she might have seen me."

"Asha, get your ass up. I'll handle Tink if the shit gets out."

"Fuck you. I'm stayin' down here."

"If that's what the fuck you want to do. You the one gone have a crook in your damn neck. Just make sure you stretch that shit out so you can suck this dick properly," he said as he grabbed his crotch.

A short trip later, we were in the room at the Downtown Courtyard. Dameon had entered first and I snuck in seconds later, hoping no one had seen me. It wasn't that I was afraid of Tink. I didn't fear no bitch. It was the fact that deep down, I knew that fucking Dameon was some scandalous ass shit. I had a feeling that I would soon be in search of a new hair Stylist. But I was a hoe and like Dameon had said…he was a paying customer.

Shonni

Chapter 11

Yawning, I walked into the kitchen to fix me a cup of coffee —Starbucks' Expresso Roast blend. Even when it came to coffee, I settled for nothing but the best. I was living better in The Projects than most outside the projects. My sponsors—Nic, Dale and Manson—kept my paper stacked and my closet packed. As Meek Mill says, I'm a Boss! I smiled to myself, pouring water into the coffee maker and inhaling the aroma of the roasted beans as the dark liquid drizzled into the coffee pot.

Waiting for the coffee to finish brewing, my thoughts traveled back to Asha, she was cool as shit. I could only wonder if it weren't for Neil, would I too be caught up and out on the Ave selling my pussy for what I considered pocket change. Then there was the Carly chick, Dream told us she was making movies in the bathroom. They said she was sucking one nigga off while another was giving it to her from behind. And another lined up waiting his turn. *This slut has no morals,* I thought—without much room to talk. Admittedly, I didn't live the life of the most virtuous woman but she was on some other shit—some freak-filled shenanigans that my conscience just wouldn't allow me to do. *At least I have some respect for myself,* I thought, clearly in denial.

I plopped down on the couch—pushing the red power button on the remote and wondering what day of the week Nic was going to schedule the delivery of my new flat screen. *Thinkin' of the devil.* As I flicked through the channels, I stopped on News Channel 6 when I spotted a photo of Nic's face flash across the television screen. It wasn't unusual to see him in the news being that he was a lawyer that handled some high-profile cases. I turned the volume up.

"Attorney Dominic T. Massea of Hockessin unexpectedly died outside the courthouse today. It is believed that the suffered from a massive heart attack. He was respected throughout the community and known as a fair person, a loving father and husband..." the short-haired brunette anchor reported.

"Turning to other news." Her voice faded away as I selfishly thought about my future without Nic's sponsorship. Dale and Manson weren't as generous with their money as Nic had been. They covered the basics; rent, lights, water, cable, insurance and a new handbag here and shopping sprees there. Nic supported my lifestyle; diamonds and designer shit. I clutched my heart, aloof to the coffee-filled mug that was in my right hand. It slipped from my grasp and collided with the surface of my new couch. Coffee splashed across the couch in every direction. There was nothing Resolve could do to eliminate the stain. It was ruined…for life.

* * *

Looking like, I belonged on the cover of Elle girl, tits up and ass out, I stepped off of the elevator into the double glass doors of the Massea Law Firm wearing a low-cut white top, a no-room-for-air black pencil skirt, red patent leather stilettos, a matching red clutch and red accessories. A phone call wasn't going to suffice in this situation. Nic may have been dead and gone, but I needed to make sure that my money still flowed in from his estate as scheduled—on the 1st and 15th of every month and not a day later.

"I'm here to see Dale Peterson," I said to the Latina chick behind the receptionist desk.

"Ya name?" She said in broken English.

Ya? Her ass must have just crossed the border. "Shon Anderson."

"Kon Anderson?"

"No. SHON," I stressed, loud and clear.

"Shun?"

I dropped my head in frustration.

If she couldn't talk the bitch could sure read expressions.

She understood perfectly and led the way to Dale's office. His door was closed. Each step closer, we could hear the chattering of voices coming from behind it. She knocked. He didn't answer. She knocked again, louder and with more force. "Mr. Peterson, you have a visitor."

The door opened. "Vera, I am in the middle of a meeting," Dale said, assertively and nothing like the shy and introverted man I believed him to be. His eyes darted from Vera to me. "Shonni, what are you doing here?"

"Dale, we need to talk. It's about…"

He interrupted me. "It's about your cousin. I'm so sorry for…"

"My cousin?" I asked, forgetting the little white lie that I had told Dale about Nic and I being related.

"Nic Massea?" Dale said, confused.

In what seemed like a flash, a woman looking like a million-bucks and counting, appeared in Dale's shadow. She was dressed to kill in a tailored, black Gucci pants suit—I knew my designers like I knew the back of my hand. And, although clearly not her own, her auburn hair flowed in soft waves down her back and over her shoulders. Except for the heavy concealer under the eyes, her make-up appeared flawless. She was draped in diamonds from head to toe—right down to the crystal studded Christian Louboutin's on her feet. *My eyes have got to be playin' tricks on me.* After a triple take, I realized exactly who she was—Laura, Nic's wife. While Nic had passed on, she looked like she had risen from the dead with a new look and the attitude to match.

"Now, tell me who this is again?" She asked Dale, swinging her extensions.

"She's Nic's cousin...your cousin-in-law?" he said, sounding and looking even more confused than before.

"Dale, darling, I believe you're mistaken," she said, eerily calmly. "She's not my husband's cousin. She's his whore," she smiled. And that's when I launched at her. Dale jumped in between us while a dark man grabbed Laura by her waist and pulled her back into Dale's office. He, too, had been in the meeting with the two of them.

"Oooohhh, 'dis is loco," Vera said, mixing languages.

"I'm sure you have work to do," Dale said, prompting her to return to her receptionist duties. "Now, the both of you need to just calm down."

"I don't have to do shit," I fixed my twisted skirt. "But what you need to do is make sure I still get my checks," mean mugging Dale.

"You must be referring to the measly five-thousand dollars that Nic's been giving you every month...twenty-five hundred on the 1st and the 15th, right?" While Laura had only been playing the fool, I was turning out to be one. "You'll probably want to start searching for another captain to save you because Nic's money is now my money."

"Bitch, please. I know Nic left me some stacks," I said, unsure but hopeful that Nic saw fit to include me in his will. After all, I could have easily ruined his career and marriage long ago with our dirty little secrets.

"Really? Well, Shonni Anderson meet my attorney, Michael Thomas."

"How the hell you know my last name?" I asked with my hands on my hips.

"Oh, I know all about you. Maybe even more than you know about yourself. And I have photos too. The ones I showed to Nic...not just of you and him but of you and Dale." Dale looked stunned. "And of you and Manson. And of you and Neil-the Mayor." *This bitch knows all of my business...must've hired a private investigator.* "And to think that Nic was actually going to leave you a quarter of a million dollars before he found out how big of a hoe you really are."

Laura had verbally sucker punched me in my gut. She turned her attention to her attorney. "Now, Michael, please inform Ms. Anderson that the two million dollars in cash, assets and property that Nic left behind belongs to me and our children and that her name is nowhere mentioned in his last will and testament."

"Ms. Anderson, I'm afraid that Mrs. Massea is right."

Nic didn't leave me two pennies to rub together. *All that fuckin' for nuthin'.*

* * *

I was down to chump change, a couple of thousand, that wouldn't last long on my caviar diet and I refused to return to eating tuna fish out of the can—literally. On those days and nights that my mother had sunk into a deep depression and rarely slid out of bed, not even for a bowel movement, I had Chicken of the Sea for breakfast, lunch and dinner. To this day, the smell of tuna sickened me as did the thought of giving up my hood rich lifestyle and returning to life below the poverty line.

My team of sponsors were dissipating fast. Neil had found out about Nic, thanks to his wife. He threatened to have my Unit and kids taken if I breathed a word about our affair. Nic was dead and Dale wasn't returning my calls. I had been blowing his phone up since leaving his office. Manson, had been missing in action. I didn't understand how he had a heart attack he wasn't even in his forties yet.

"Have a yard sale," Asha said, sitting as far away from the coffee stain on my couch as she could while I paced my living room floor in deep thought.

"Bitch bye, I ain't about to see bitches walkin' around The Bridges rockin' my shit."

Asha had become my new best friend. She barely ever stayed at her house due to the memories of Cream and the detectives were still snooping around trying to get answers.

"You got tons of clothes with the price tags still attached," Asha said, indirectly suggesting that I make a "return" trip to the mall.

"I don't know what I'm goin' to do. I'll think of somethin'."

"Well, you know I'm livin' trick-to-trick but if I had it, I would give it."

Asha left me to wallow in my misery alone. Not since I was sixteen-years-old layin' up in the Courtyard while Neil humped on me had I stressed about money. *Remember,* I thought to myself. *As long as there are niggas to be fucked...there's money to be made.* I dialed Manson. In addition to paying my rent and utility bills, I needed him to splurge for my car insurance next month since Dale had clearly kicked me to the curb.

"Shonni," Manson said, picking up on the first ring.

"Hey, Daddy," I said, seductively.

"I was just thinkin' 'bout you. How you holdin' up since your *cousin* is gone?"

I looked at the phone something wasn't right about his tone.

"I've been good, a little shaken up, but I'm ok. I miss you Daddy," I said, trying to skip the subject. "Why don't you come over so that I can show you how much?"

"I can't."

"If not tonight, then tomorrow."

"No, Shonni. I can't...fuck wit you know more. You a lying trick bitch, Nic wasn't your fucking cousin. You lucky I'm letting you live..."

I hung up the phone.

I gulped hard and looked around in a panic. That nigga was crazy and I did not want to be on his shit list.

I called Dale out of desperation.

He answered on the second ring.

"Oh my God Dale, I need you-please come over." I begged.

"I can't..."

Now my damn ears are playin' tricks on me. "Come again."

"Shonni, I got saved."

"Huh?" I was speechless.

"I've been thinkin' 'bout you tryin' to figure out how I was goin' to tell you. I got saved and I'm tryin' to live right...be a faithful husband and a good father to my kids. I'm sorry Shonni, but I can't see you or help you out with your finances anymore. It's over."

"Why don't you save that shit for another bitch. Don't play yourself."

"Shonni, that's just it...cheating on my wife...not being around for my kids...not honoring God, playing myself is exactly what I've been doing. I don't want to be face to face with the maker only to be sentenced to eternal damnation."

Eternal damnation. This nigga sound like he is in a cult. "Dale, stop playin' and come over here so that I can give you a little piece of heaven right here on earth."

"Shonni, I'm for real and Jesus is real. You should try him."

"Try this." I clicked the phone shut in his ear, hoping it was loud enough to bust his ear drum. *Ain't this some shit?* There were no players left for me to substitute in the game. My bench was empty.

Carly

Chapter 12

"Yeah, just like that…deep throat that shit." Beef held the camcorder inches away from my face, thinking he was the black Larry Flynt.

The next two voices I heard were Dream's and the nigga Beef had paid to guard the restroom door.

"You can't go in there."

"The hell if I…" Dream was stopped dead in her tracks. "What the fuck? You a fuckin' hoe for real…like real talk…for real…like the Queen Hoe of the world." She disapprovingly shook her head and stood with her hands on her hips.

I wasn't too familiar with the Bible but somewhere in it, I know it said something about a person removing the plank out of his or her own eye before trying to take the spec out of their sister's or brother's eye. Or, as Ki-Ki put it, "Sweep around your own damn unit before you try to sweep around mine's." *They always up in my damn business,* I thought, staring back at Dream.

Coming home after the club, I followed Dream to Ms. Vett's to pick up my girls. Dream picked up her son and left not even saying bye. Synda was sprawled out on a pallet in the middle of her living room floor along with her two youngest granddaughters.

"Let her sleep. Just make sure you come get her in the mornin'. She been needing you; she upset about her daddy," Ms. Vett yawned, dragging herself to her bedroom. Instead of taking my ass home, I trailed the aroma weed to Amber's unit, who lived next door to Spirit. Amber's mother had passed away of breast cancer a few years earlier, leaving her to become the woman of the house at age thirteen. She took care of her father's and brother's needs and some in South Bridge believed she was being forced to do more than cook and clean. But, no one every reported the suspected sexual abuse. Yet, everyone was quick to call the police when it was rumored that Bucket—who lived around the block in another set of units—had a one-hundred-pound pet snake caged up in his apartment. Granted, a snake was dangerous but as many niggas as it was around the hood packing heat, I'm sure someone would have shot the animal if it had ever gotten loose.

Turns out, there never a snake; just a scare tactic that he had thought of to keep niggas from trying to break into his unit and steal his stash. It all went to show how fucked up our mentalities were in the projects; we were more consumed with the presence of a snake in our community then a family of pedophiles. However, Amber was eighteen now and I figured that if there was any truth to the matter, she would have packed up her shit and left already—that is if she had anywhere else to go.

"What's up?" She asked, sitting on the concrete steps of her unit with some tights on, a wife beater and smoking the blunt I had sniffed out.

"Not much," I said, taking a seat next to her.

"Sorry bout Cream-he was cool as shit."

"Thanks."

"You wanna hit this?"

"You know I do or I wouldn't have brought my white ass over here."

She passed the blunt to me, "Where your brother 'n 'em?"

"In the house runnin' a train on Janelli." *Good,* I thought—thinking that if Ambers' father and brothers were getting some pussy elsewhere that they weren't taking it from her.

"The Mexican chick that works for Tuffy?" I asked, passing the blunt back to her.

"Umm-hmm. She came up in here wearin' a sequenced prom dress...lookin' like they picked her up from a Quinceanera."

I laughed. "Girl, you crazy."

"Tuffy gone beat her ass when she shows back up empty handed. Them niggas ain't got no money," she said about her father and brothers.

"That's fucked up how they gone do that girl like that."

"They some dirty niggas."

In so little words, she had confirmed the worse. She had been sexually abused by the men who were supposed to protect her. And while everyone was worried about losing air to an imaginary snake, Amber had long been emotionally, mentally and physically dismembered. Only she knew why she had stayed.

"You cool?" I asked.

"I'm cool," she said. "You got any of those xannies?"

* * *

Synda came skipping home. She had syrup stuck to the side of her face. Ms. Vett had cooked breakfast; pancakes, eggs and grits. I couldn't remember the last time I had cooked breakfast. Usually, Synda fixed herself a bowl of cereal or some Instant oatmeal— when we had groceries. And to be honest, I couldn't remember the last time I cooked lunch or dinner either.

"It was good too, Carly," Synda said, full and apparently satisfied. "And Ms. Vett said Daddy in heaven with the angels looking over us and I didn't have to be sad anymore."

I walked back over to the navy Rent-A-Center couch where I had laid my head last night—too tired, drunk and high to make it any further inside my unit after leaving Amber's.

"Guess what Mama?"

"What?" I asked, lighting a cigarette.

"I saw your friend on TV."

I choked on the first drag. "What?" I coughed. "My friend?"

"Beef came over and well...they went into Kev's room and they locked the door. He left his backpack though," she said. "I told Sonny that he not supposed to be going through other people stuff, but he didn't listen to me. He looked through it anyway and found a whole bunch of movies."

"He did?" I asked, steaming.

"Yep. He found a bag of white candy too."

My heart palpitated.

"But we didn't eat any."

I breathed a sigh of release.

"He took a movie out though and we started watchin' it. The room on the TV looked just like your room and then they showed your friend's face...the man that came over the other day with the other man and there was a woman too."

My heart stopped.

"Her head was down in his private part area and it was going up and down...up and down, but you couldn't see her face. I think it was a bad movie. Sonny said it was a flic," she whispered, knowing the "movie" wasn't for a child's eyes.

Sonny ass is too grown. "Stay here."

I slipped into my house shoes and stormed over to Ms. Vett's unit. She had just finished up washing dishes from breakfast and was wiping the kitchen counters off when she came into the living room where I was questioning Kev about what Synda had told me.

"Carly," She said with a floral-print scarf tied around her head. "I know you didn't come up in my house tryin' to confront my son 'bout some shit you brought upon yourself. You must've lost your got damn mind." Her neck rolled.

"You was supposed to be watchin' Synda…."

"Shit, you be laid up wit' niggas all day long. What's the damn difference?"

"How Synda ended up watchin' a porno."

"Your ass made the decision to *make* a porno. If you were so worried about her ever watchin' it, you should have thought twice before you opened your legs for the world to see. Now, take your ass on and don't call over here ever again askin' me to babysit no damn more…got my damn blood pressure up. You worse than these damn kids around here."

"Don't worry. I won't."

I marched back to my unit, suddenly feeling a little queasy.

* * *

My arms hugged the base of the porcelain toilet bowl. I hadn't vomited as much since my first trimester carrying Synda. I knew for a fact that I wasn't simply hung over; it took more than a couple of drinks to render me deliriously drunk. *I can't be,* I thought, lifting my head up to focus on the three small circular imprints in my shoulder—sure that three months hadn't passed by since my last Depo-Provera shot. I hadn't had a period since I birthed Symia, but that was a common side effect of the shot. *Maybe it's the Botox.*

Because my lips were so thin and constantly reminded me of my mother's lips, I frequently injected them with Botox that I ordered from the Internet. But, to be honest, if someone put a syringe full of Botox in front of me and another filled with saline solution, I wouldn't be able to decipher the difference. Cream had warned me. "You dumb as shit...injectin' yourself with some shit that you got from off the Internet...a medical spa in Guatemala...some shit that ain't FDA approved," she had said. But, I wasn't one to take heed to warnings.

With one hand on the bathroom counter and another on the tub, I managed to stand to my feet. Taking baby steps, I walked over to the sink and rinsed the vomit residue out of my mouth. *Gross.* I wiped my face on a hand towel and drug myself into my bedroom, resting on the edge of my unmade bed.

"Synda, honey?" I used the little energy I had to call on her.

"Huh?"

"What?"

"I mean…yes, Ma'am?"

That's more like it. "Can you bring Mama her purse, please?"

Seconds later, she came running down the hall with my imitation Coach bag that I had copped from Cowtown.

"Thanks, baby."

"You okay, Mama."

"Yes, baby, Mama's fine. Just a little sick."

"Okay," Synda said, racing back to the living room to watch her beloved cartoons.

I emptied all of the contents of my purse onto my bed, searching for the business card I had to Henrietta Johnsons Clinic. They were usually open on Saturdays, but I wasn't for sure how long. Shit, as much fucking as I did lately, I should have had the clinic on speed dial. I found the card amongst old receipts from K&F Store and Rainbow. I flipped my phone open but instead of a dial tone, I heard two niggas on the other end arguing over whether or not Kim Kardashian's ass was real.

"Nigga, I seen that shit on Mediatakeout.com. One of her booty pads had slid all the way down to the back of her knee. It was stuck right inside the crease. They showed a picture of that shit. I'm tellin' you her ass ain't real."

"Fuck you, nigga. Her ass is real."

Dumb and Dumber. It was Beef and Pop.

"Hello!"

"Yo', Carly. I copped a spot for us to film another scene at. It's gone be another hot set-up. Pop and me on our way. We gone come scoop you up."

"I can't..."

"There you go with that bullshit."

"Nigga, I'm fuckin' sick to my damn stomach so unless you want me hurlin' all over your dick...give me a couple of days."

"Yo'...I just got this spot for tonight. So you need to do whatever you need to do to feel better...drink a glass of water and take a nap, but be ready in two hours."

"Nigga, what the fuck drinkin' a glass of water gone do."

"I dunno that's just what my mama always told me to do when I was sick."

I remained silent, staring up and the popcorn ceiling in my unit and rolling my eyes.

"Carly...Carly...I know this bitch didn't hang up on me," he said, talking to Pop.

"Carly…"

"Nigga, what?" I finally answered him.

"Bitch, be ready when I blow the horn."

Asha

Chapter 13

There was very little in life that my eyes hadn't seen nor ears hadn't heard—from identifying Lynn's decomposing body down at the county morgue to having no choice but to listen to her fuck Trick after Trick in our tiny apartment in which the walls were so paper-thin that the cotton balls that I had stuffed in my ears were worthless.

With such childhood memories following me into the life I lived as a prostitute, I had come to expect the unexpected. From one trick requesting that I spank his bare ass with a wooden paddle and pretend that I was his third grade teacher punishing him to thug-ass niggas asking me to fuck them in the butt hole with a strap on. Those tricks always paid me extra—not for the request but to keep their dirty little secrets...secret.

But the events that had transpired between Dameon and I were un-fucking-believable. When I left the Courtyard, he was knocked out cold. I did what I had to do and left the hotel room with my money, burying the entire night into the back of my head.

A thousand dollars richer than I was before I decided to take a few days off and sleep never felt so good. It had been a long time since I had closed my eyes without the dread of waking up to tackle another night on the Ave. And I was in a deep sleep, slobbering all over my pillow, until someone—knocking on my door like the damn DEA about to conduct a drug bust—awakened me. I jumped up, catching a glimpse at the clock. It was half past noon, dead smack in the middle of the summer—too hot for niggas in the projects to be casually out and about if they weren't hustling. And broads were still under the covers if they didn't have a hair, nail or WIC appointment. And needless to say, girl scouts didn't dare come near the concrete jungle trying to sell boxes of Thin Mints and Samoas. *Can't be nobody but them damn Jehovah Witnesses.* They were some brave souls...*Gotta be them.*

Usually, I avoided their asses by not answering the door, but I had a mouth full for them for waking me up out of my sleep. Without peeking through the living room blinds or looking through the peephole, I swung the door open—with my hands on my hips and my neck ready to roll.

"Who the hell done pissed you off?" Ki-Ki asked. "And what the fuck is that white shit on your jaw?"

She stared at the crusted slob stuck to the side of my face. "You need to get a wash rag and wipe that mess off." She brushed past me and into my unit. As usual, she was greased down in Vaseline and doused in Muslim oil. She had on a tank top, cut off jean shorts, some off fresh Pumas with ankle socks with the fuzz ball on the back. She had a drawer full in every color. The first and only time that I ever questioned her about her obsession, she cussed me out for forty-three minutes straight without taking a breath.

"I'm a grown ass woman. I wear what the fuck I wanna wear. I ain't said shit about you wearin' them short ass spandex dresses...showin' your ass cheeks and trickin on Cash Ave. Do you and I'll do me," she snapped.

Damn. I stole a glance in the mirror hanging above my couch. A trail of dried up slob ran from the crease of my mouth up the side of my face and damn near to my ear.

"I bet Ray Charles could see that shit from a mile away," Ki-Ki laughed.

"You ain't right," I shook my head, refusing to laugh. If I was going to hell, it was going to be for not treating my body like a temple as the Bible suggested; not for making a mockery of the disabled.

"You know that shit was funny," Ki-Ki said, entering my kitchen. "What you got to drink?" She opened up my refrigerator. "Can I have a Coke?"

115

Before I could give her permission, she picked up a can and dropped it in her bag. The bag had her name bedazzled in rhinestones on the side of it. Now, that shit was funny. *Where the hell did she find a bedazzler?* But, I kept my thoughts to myself. The last thing I wanted to do was give her another reason to go all-the-way to the left on me again.

"You goin' shoppin?" I asked.

"You know it."

"You startin' early today, ain't you?"

"Gotta get my hustle on...I just stopped by to tell you that some nigga came by K&F lookin' for you."

Fuck. There was either a pussy-whipped trick stalking me or Dameon had sent someone to kill me. I had to pull out my stun gun and use it on his ass— literally. That nigga had the audacity to ask me if he could pee in my mouth. There wasn't shit in the world, including money that a nigga could offer me that would entice me into letting a motherfucker pee in my mouth. After turning down his request, Dameon attacked me—pinning me down and shoving his dick in my face. Luckily, my bag was within arm's length on the hotel nightstand. I grabbed my taser and let it off up the crack of his ass, electrocuting him into a state of unconsciousness. "Nasty nigga." I kicked him in his side as he lay motionless on the floor. "Got me fucked up."

Ki-Ki went on, describing the man on the hunt for me. "He was big…more fat than muscular with giant rolls of sausage links in the back of his head."

"What did he say his name was?" I asked.

"He didn't…said he'd stop by again today."

"That's strange."

"Just have your taser ready when he comes knockin' again," Ki-Ki warned me, walking out the door.

I had just used it hours earlier and had no problems using it again if the situation required it.

* * *

Trying to fall back asleep was a losing effort. One, I couldn't stop wondering about the identity of the mystery man looking for me. And two, there was another knock on my door shortly after Ki-Ki left.

I reached in my bag and grabbed my stun gun, slowing cracking the door open.

"Can I help you?"

"You Asha?"

"Who's askin'?"

He made a facial expression that read *I don't have time for this shit*. "Blair sent me."

"Blair?"

"Yeah, he sent me to find you and deliver you to him."

Blair was still in town. Deliver. If I had no idea where he was staying, I would have stuffed myself in a cardboard box and Fed Ex'd my damn self to him. *And just as I was beginning to believe that I was just a passerby in his life.*

"Wait…I can't go with you," I said, feeling all of the joy I had just experienced simply thinking about seeing Blair seep out of me like air from a nail-inflected tire.

"Hold on," he said, reaching for his cell phone. "Yeah, man…I found her. She lives in East Bridge. He paused. "Cool." He clicked his cell phone shut. "Blair said he needs to see you."

"Okay, give me a few seconds." I didn't want to keep the man waiting, but I couldn't let Blair see me looking a hot damn mess. I had on some oversized gray sweats, a stained t-shirt and my hair wrapped in a scarf. "It's gonna be more like thirty minutes."

"Cool. I'll be waitin' in the car."

Forty-five minutes later, I stepped out of my unit and into the backseat of a silver Bentley sitting on twenty-four inch rims. As we coasted away, my phone rang.

"Umm- whose car did I just see you get into?" It was Shonni.

Nosy ass. "A friend's."

"A friend? What kind of friend drives two-hundred-thousand dollar cars?"

"The kind you need right about now." I joked. I looked back at Shonni's unit and saw her peeking through her blinds. "I gotta go."

"Asha, don't hang…"

I hung up, sat back and enjoyed the ride.

* * *

Two hours later we pulled up at the National Harbor outside of D.C. This was the first time I had ever been this far down. I sat up in my seat and peered out the window at all of the boutique shops and grand hotels. People of all races littered the streets shopping and taking in the sites. We pulled up in front a hotel and resort called the Gaylord National Conventional Center. I had never seen a hotel so big.

Buff—my nickname for our chauffer—put the Bentley in park, hopped out and tossed the keys to the valet worker who looked scared to death to take the wheel of the expensive car.

"Don't let me see a scratch on my shit when I come back to pick it up," Buff said, making matters worse. "I'll serve your own ass to you on a shish kabob with some green peppers and onions." *Hungry ass,* I thought. *Try servin' him them sausage links in the back of your head.*

Buff led me inside we entered a huge atrium that resembled a mall. We went passed the Belvedere Lounge Bar, it reminded me of the piano bars you would see the old Hollywood starlet sing in at the movies. Rooms with balconies were on three sides of the walls. The front wall was made of glass; it reminded me somewhat of a green house. We entered the elevator and got off on the 7th floor. The sign said, Exterior –View Presidential Suite. Buff opened the doors and all I could say was "Wow!" I stood in awe of the 2,788 square foot suite. My unit could fit inside the suite six times. There was a kitchen, bar, living room, formal dining room, den, conference room, bay window overlooking the Potomac River and Woodrow Wilson Bridge. Shonni's unit was hot but this shit right here was *Boss*.

"Boss Man," Buff peeked his head into the suite's conference room. "You're guest is here."

"Show her to the master bedroom and tell Asha to make herself at home. I have some business to finish up. Tell her I'll be out shortly."

From the foyer where I was standing, I could see into the conference room. I didn't see Blair but got an eye full of a group of men dressed in suits and ties seated in black leather chairs at a large cherry wood table. Whoever Blair was and whatever he did, the title came with money, power and respect.

Suddenly, I felt unworthy; not good enough, smart enough, beautiful enough or deserving of being in the presence of such exquisiteness. I physically resided in the projects and had also mentally confined myself there too.

I plopped down on the plush bed in the master bedroom, feeling like a destitute project chick. My eyes watered. I was who I was; some orphaned girl, raised in project housing with a prostitute for a mother figure, and a broken dream of one day becoming more than my mother had turned out to be.

There was a knock on the bedroom door.

"Come in," I sniffled and dried up my watery eyes.

My God. I felt my heart drop at the sight of Blair. *Damn, he's fine as hell!* He wasn't wearing the Rock-out Mega trap star assemble that he rocked when we first met; he was dressed in a nice pair of black slacks that draped over a pair of black, squared-toed shoes. The sleeves on his Oxford shirt were rolled up to his elbows and his tie hung loosely around his neck. He looked like he belonged on Wall Street.

"Asha," he turned his attention to me. "You're a hard woman to catch up with. Cedric told me that he searched high and low for you the other night. He said there was some type of homicide that happened in front of your house. I was concerned. Are you ok?"

"Well, Cedric must have not looked too hard, you know where I be. As for the situation at my unit. As you can see I'm good. It's over and it doesn't' matter anymore."

"As long as you are all right is what matters to me…we'll discuss where you *be* later." Blair smiled. "You hungry?"

121

Dinner was served in the formal dining room of the suite. Similar to the setting and aura of a five-star restaurant. Amongst the amenities, the presidential suite also came equipped with its' own personal chef and waiter. For the evening, I was living the lifestyle of the rich and famous. *I could get use to this.*

With our hunger tamed, we headed to the living room where we watched The Purge 3 on the 72" flat screen mounted on the wall. However, seconds into the movie, I fell asleep and so did Blair. The credits were rolling when I opened my eyes again. I stared at Blair, his chest heaving up and down in a slow and steady pace. The only time that I had seen the ocean was on old episodes of Bay Watch, but I had been on the corner plenty of times to catch the sun rising. And Blair was as beautiful and breathtaking as both. He stirred and his eye lids fluttered open.

"What time is it?" He stretched.

"I don't know. I just woke up myself." I yawned.

"Come here." He gestured for me to join him on his end of the couch.

There were too many thoughts running through my mind. First and foremost, I did not want him to get a close up of my sew-in. Secondly, although he hadn't made any sexual advances towards me, I wasn't for sure what he was expecting if anything. I scooted down on the couch. Blair wrapped his arms around me. Before I could inform him that nothing was about to go down between the two of us, his lips brushed my earlobe. The warmth of his breath sent chills down my body. I had never been so close to a man without the intention of screwing him for money. "I don't think you know how special you are," he whispered in my ear.

"Why didn't you tell Cedric where he could have easily found me?" I asked, ignoring the statement he had made because at the time, no one had ever made me feel special or ever told me that I was.

"Because I wanted him to pick you up like a gentleman would a lady...at her front door...not from off the Ave."

I broke loose from Blair's arms.

"What's wrong?"

"You can't seem to get it. I'm a hoe...a prostitute. I sell ass for cash. My aunt did it her whole life and so did other members of my family. Guess it was what I was born to do," I said, remembering our encounter at the Dupont Hotel when he asked me why I dressed the way I did.

"Asha." Blair sat up on the couch. "Do you really believe what you are saying'? Do you hear yourself?"

"I don't know who you are or what you want from me, but if you can't accept me for who I am, I'm out!" I had so much anger inside and I had no idea why I was taking it out on him-he didn't deserve it.

"I like you, Asha. There's something about you that I'm drawn to. I only want to help you, but it's your decision if you want to remain at the bottom or rise to the top. I'm offering you an opportunity to turn your life around." Blair stood up. "Cedric will be up and ready to take you back home in the morning. Think about what I said. A friend of mine will be in contact with you soon to see what you have decided."

Blair disappeared into one of the suite's other rooms. He left me on the couch to contemplate my destiny and wonder if he was sincere. My mind had been poisoned and the words that I heard time and time again taunted me, "You can't turn a Hoe into a housewife." Could Blair really be way out of this dreadful situation?

𝔖𝔥𝔬𝔫𝔫𝔦

𝔠𝔥𝔞𝔭𝔱𝔢𝔯 14

President and CEO. I studied the business card in my hand. The gloss coated finish with detailed custom graphics was a sure sign that it was printed professionally and not on a home computer. Bob was the nigga I had met in the frozen food aisle at Food Lion. He was tall, lanky and brown skin. And according to his business card, he owned an international textiles and merchandising company. *International?* If Bob's company was international, that meant he was getting money from all over the globe. *A bitch is back in business.*

"Bob?"

"Yeah."

"This is Shonni. I met you at Food Lion," I made sure I gave him my seductive business swag.

"All yeah...beauty with a booty, What's good?"

"I was..." My response was abruptly halted by noise in the background—kids crying and a woman—his wife I suppose—trying to calm them down. "Bob!"

I heard her yell. "Can you please help me with the triplets?" *Triplets?* He put me on hold.

"Sorry about that. I'm back. What were you sayin'?"

"I was wonderin' if you wanted to come over. We could have dinner by candlelight and you could have me for dessert."

"Damn, it's that easy?"

"Only for you, boo."

"Just let me know when and where and I'm there." Bob didn't think twice about his wife and kids and neither did I.

* * *

Hearing a car door slam, I jumped up and looked out the window. *I know that ain't Bob's car.* He was driving a beat-up Crown Vic with some prehistoric Five Star rims on it. *Maybe he drivin' that car as a decoy...scared that niggas in hood might rob him or somethin' if he drove his real ride. Yeah...that's it,* I convinced myself. But then, I was confronted with another shocker as Bob stepped out of the car and walked up my sidewalk. He was wearing a pair of jeans starched stiff with creases in them dangerous enough to decapitate somebody. *Who the hell wears creases in their jeans nowadays?* I contemplated not answering the door. Unlike the excuse I had conjured about his car to console myself, there was nothing that could be said to excuse those weapons of mass destruction pressed into his pants. His swagger or lack there off was throwing me for a loop, but I quickly reminded myself that just because a nigga had money didn't mean he automatically had swag.

"I got these on fourth street the Mexicans practically gave these shits away." He handed me a bouquet of dying roses.

"I see," I said, staring at the dirty clear cellophane the roses were bundled in.

"Damn, you look good."

"Thanks," I said, halfheartedly. Suddenly I felt like a bitch did when she got dressed to the nines for a date only to come home feeling like she had wasted an outfit. And my gut was telling me that by the end of the night, I was going to regret ever calling Bob in the first place.

"It smells good up in here too."

"Thanks." *There goes that halfhearted smile again.*

"I didn't know y'all was livin' like this over here in projects," he said, looking around my unit. "Me and wifey need to get one of these joints, this shit right here is fresher than a mother fucka."

"*Everybody* ain't," I said, ignoring the rest of his slick ass comment.

Over dinner, Bob and I didn't talk about much. *As long as he understands dollars and cents.* He gobbled down the hearty meal of steak and potatoes that I had cooked. He sucked particles of food out of his teeth

127

like a teenager with braces. *How disgusting?* I endured Bob for one reason and one reason only—because he owned his own company and I needed to rebuild my team of sponsors.

Knowing he was ready for "dessert," I stalled and decided to hand wash our dirty dishes along with the others in the sink as opposed to placing them in the dishwasher. He walked up behind me, placing his hands on my hips and running his tongue up and down the nape of my neck. I wasn't turned on in the least, especially with the creases in his damn jeans slicing into the back of my legs.

"I'm ready for dessert," he said as I had predicted he would.

"If I give you some, what you gone do for me?"

"I'll take care of you. Don't worry, boo I got you."

Just the words I wanted to hear. He slid his hands up my dress. "Oh shit, you ain't got no panties on." He raised my dress up. "Damn, look at that ass. It's beautiful." He bent me over the kitchen sink and the tip of his tongue slipped in between my ass crack. *Damn.* His tongue in my ass felt great. Simultaneously, he jammed his fingers in my pussy. My oils were dripping down my leg onto the kitchen floor.

"You're so wet," he moaned, unbuckling his belt.

"Make sure you wrap it up."

Five minutes later, Bob was hunched over my back trying to catch his breath. "You the fuckin' best," he said.

"The best you ever had?"

"By far the best."

"Better than your wife?" I asked, discreetly suggesting to him that what he had at home couldn't compare.

"Way better."

He rose up off my back and pulled his pants up from his ankles while I pulled my dress back down over my exposed ass.

"So, what kind of business do you have exactly? What does textiles and merchandising mean?" I asked, a little too late.

"Ugh...well...you know...I basically have my own clothin' line," He stuttered.

"Your own *clothing* line?

"Yeah, right now I'm waitin' on some fabrics from Italy because I'm doin' a men's suit collection."

"Waiting on?"

"Yeah, you know the line is in the beginnin' stages of conception. I'm still pickin' out fabrics."

"But do you have some suits in stores now...Nordstrom's, Macy's...Neiman's?"

"No-no, not yet. Right now, I just got these t-shirts that I be sellin' down at Cowtown."

"T-shirts? Cowtown? Is that all!" I was about to be sick.

"I park my car at my man's barber shop and pop open the trunk on Market Street too. I got all the hot tees."

"Nigga, you tellin' me you the t-shirt man?"

"That's me!"

I didn't even respond. He read the expression on my face.

"I got a day job though. I'm the manager over at Wawa."

"Wawa?" *What the fuck was in it for me-free hoagies?* "Get out!" I screamed.

"What?"

"I said, get the fuck out!" I picked up the vase with the roses he had given me in it. "Get out before I crack your skull to the white meat."

"What did I do?"

"It's not what you did but who you *ain't*. Now, get your lyin' ass out of my house."

"You crazy as shit. My mom was right about you Spanish bitches!" he said, hurrying out the door.

"Yeah, I'm insane for fucking you for free!" I screamed again, aiming the vase at his head. It missed and crashed onto the sidewalk. "And I'm not Spanish-I'm bi-racial!"

Broken glass was everywhere, reminding me of how my father had shattered my mother's heart. When he committed suicide, I didn't know who to hate more—him or her; Him for causing her so much heartache because he wanted to take the easy way out, or her because she felt like she couldn't live without him and buried herself in her jobs forgetting that she had children. I was a grown ass woman who knew the difference between right and wrong; moral and immoral. But there was no denying it, the hate I had for both my mother and father led me to allow money to guide the direction of my life instead of love. It was why I was in the situation I was in.

* * *

Feeling down on my luck, I headed over to Ms. Vett's like the others in the projects I was now looking at her as a surrogate mother. She wasn't Oprah and her advice tended to be unconventional to some. But, she had lived and learned—the hard way.

Ms. Vett's unit smelled like the green Fabuloso and bleach. To have as many children, including mine, in and out of her unit, she managed to keep her unit extremely clean.

"I don't play that livin' foul shit-honey," she always said. "If you gone live with me there's two things you gone keep clean…my house and yo' own ass."

"Hey, y'all."

The kids were all piled up in the living room playing Xbox connects. My boys ran over to me and gave me hugs and kisses. This was a first. My oldest, Sonny whispered in my ear, "Can we come home now," I nodded my head. It was time.

"Hey Ms. Vett..." I walked into the kitchen where she was writing her numbers down to be played.

"Grandma..." Sonny came running into the kitchen.

"Yes baby?"

"You cookin' a cake too?" He asked, with his fingers crossed.

"I got some Jiffy cornbread in the oven. It tastes just like cake. Now, go back in the livin' room...so I can talk with your mother." He skipped away. She turned her attention to me. "What the hell is wrong with you?"

"Hi to you too...Nothin' is wrong with me. What you talkin' about?"

"I'm talkin' 'bout why look so damn sad."

I laughed. "Well, if you didn't already know I had a couple of bad days."

I told her about Nic's wife, about Neil and Manson both cutting me loose, about Dale finding the Lord, I even told her about Bob's lame ass.

"First of all, when a nigga hands you his business card, the first thing you need to be checkin' for is his company's federal identification number. That's how you know a he's legit. Secondly, maybe you need to redefine your definition of who you believe a Boss is to be."

"Redefine?"

"A boss by your standards is a woman who is basically dependent on a man or in your case...men...to take care of her. And I heard you like to say that shit about as long as there's niggas to be fucked then there's money to be made. But, hell, you gotta fuck a herd of niggas before you come across a nigga with bank. You lucked up on Nic, Neil, Dale and Manson."

"So, what you sayin'?"

"I'm sayin' a boss is really a woman who's got her own."

Ms. Vett was right. I needed to find a way to "get my own" that didn't necessarily involve me letting a nigga get between my thighs. But change didn't come quick or easy. It never did. I left Ms. Vett's in search of Heedy, hoping that the three grand he had offered me to entertain Man-Man's Haitian connect was still up for grabs. After this, no more...I was picking up my kids and working on getting my own.

Carly

Chapter 15

Getting myself into sticky situations was easy, getting out of them was another story. Beef didn't seem to think that he could find another white girl to exploit or one like me who turned big tricks on a promissory note. *Cash up front.* That was Asha's motto—one that I should've adopted. *How did I get myself into this shit?* The more important question was; how was I going to get out? I had gone from being a whore without a pimp to a low-budget porn star with two pimps. Survival in the hood or outside of it was achievable without a bitch having to stoop so low.

* * *

Beef and Pop were fifteen minutes away. I wasn't feeling any better, but I had managed to pull myself together. However, I didn't have a babysitter and as I figured she would, Synda wanted to stay with me at my mom's.

"Dosha…you said to stay with her for a few hours. Can't you?" I asked Synda, who had a sour look on her face.

"No!" She crossed her arms and rolled her eyes. I felt a tantrum coming on—it was the white in her.

"Why not?"

"She breathes too loud and it scares me."

I couldn't help but laugh. Kids noticed everything. Dosha *had* been diagnosed with a breathing disorder but she continued to chain smoke, drink and she was overweight. She was a glimpse of me in the future if I didn't quit smoking.

"How about Spirit?"

"No!"

"Am…" I cut my damn self-off. There was no way I was letting Synda near Amber's father or brothers.

"I want to stay with Ms. Vett or Asha!" She said, stomping her little feet.

Deep down, I truly believed that Ms. Vett owed me an apology but, I decided to be the bigger person and apologize to her. Asha, the one who is the reason I have to bury my baby daddy is out! I wanted to slap the shit outta Synda. Had she forgotten about her dead daddy already? Honestly it seemed like Creams death was irrelevant to everybody, including his family. No one called me to check on his kids or anything. Syncere was still M.I.A-shit was crazy. Synda and I marched over to Ms. Vett's, I apologized and to my surprise, she agreed to babysit. I knew it was only because of her soft spot for Synda.

The backseat of Pop's car was stuffed full of miscellaneous items; boxes of jewelry, clothes, shoes, electronics, DVD's, CD's, tools, household appliances and other shit. *What the hell...a garage sale on wheels?* I left the matter alone and squeezed into the car. It was a tight fit—so tight that I had to sit sideways. To make matters worse, it was hot as hell and his backseat windows didn't roll down. They were broken. I knew this wasn't his real car. Ms. Vett bragged about all the degrees and the good job that he had. I couldn't tell he was always on some shit on the low. I heard he was a major distributor of pills in Rosegate. There was no telling with Beef's ass.

"Can you please turn on the air? My make-up gone sweat off by the time we get to where we're goin'."

"The air don't work." *Don't shit in this motherfucker work.* "Your face gone be blurred on the DVD's so it don't matter. Here," he handed me a yellow Wendy's napkin.

"What am I supposed to do with this?"

"Fan yourself."

"With a napkin?"

It was clear, neither Beef or Pop gave a fuck and I think this was a joke to them. They were too busy running their mouths to notice the blacked-out Chevy Suburban that had been tailing us since we screeched out of the Projects in Pop's beat-up Sentra. We had made a few stops but were now on I-95. Pop swerved into the middle lane. The suburban did the same. *Yep. We're bein' followed.*

Thirty minutes later, we exited the highway and drove miles into the Greenville the suburbs of Wilmington. The spacious SUV was still on our tail; a few cars back. *Speak up or forever hold your peace.* I decided to hold my peace and let the night proceed as it was destined to.

Pop dimmed the lights on the car and glided it through an open steel gate. A brick two-story mini-mansion rested at the end of the long driveway that we had pulled into. The house was exquisite but—by far—wasn't the largest and or most luxurious home in the area. Anyone who was someone lived in Greenville; business men, high-profile politicians and even actors and actresses.

It looked as if no one was home. There were no cars in the driveway or any lights that appeared to be on and the neighboring houses were acres away. Before exiting the Neon, Beef handed Pop and I a pair of gloves; not plastic gloves, but some hot ass cotton mittens.

"What the hell?"

"Just put them on."

We approached the front door. Beef reached into his jean pocket but instead of pulling out a key, he pulled out the same pocket knife that he had used to threaten my life with at The Grey House. *Shiesty ass nigga,* I thought, for sure that the alarm would sound. It didn't. Come to find out, Pop's sister was a dispatcher at ADT and had disengaged the alarm. Beef jimmied the door open with ease.

Inside, we were greeted by a grand marble foyer. A round oak wood table rested in the middle of the entrance and was topped with a vase full of blooming lilies. Two stair cases—one on each side of the foyer—led to the second floor of the home. To the right was the formal living room. I walked over to the fireplace. The mantle was overflowing with picture frames showcasing the smiles and memories of a happy family; a mother, father, two teenage sons and a younger daughter.

"Where y'all at?" I heard Beef on his cell phone, which I assumed was stolen since he and Pop were turning out to be nothing more than petty thieves. *Entrepreneurs-Yeah, right? I had been sold a dream, but it wasn't the first time.* I thought about Man-Man. "Y'all were supposed to be right behind us," Beef said. I figured he was talking to the driver of the suburban. I had made much to do about nothing.

"Here." Beef threw a plastic bag from Party City at me. It was full of costumes; a black-and-white maid's outfit, a white-and-red nurse's ensemble, a blue stewardess' get-up and a shirt-and-short set that resembled a police uniform. "We gone shoot four scenes tonight," he said as the doorbell rang.

Two niggas the color of a shiny new penny walked in and they looked just as flawless as one too. *Twins.* They were identical—one just an inch or two shorter than the other but equally fine with football-player physics. There was something genuine about them. They weren't gangsta niggas and they seemed clueless about selling drugs, pimping hoes or robbing people. They were just two horny ass boys that Beef and Pop and promised some free pussy.

"We had to stop by the liquor store to get this party started right," the taller twin said, gripping a brown paper sack.

"Who the fuck are they?" I asked.

"Your co-workers for the night," Beef said and I knew exactly what he meant.

"No!" I crossed my arms in protest as Synda had done earlier. "I ain't fuckin' them niggas. I don't even know them."

Beef cut his eyes at me with a bitch-please look on his face. "Since when have you had to know a nigga before fuckin' him?"

"Since right now. I'm out of here." I tried to push past Beef. He grabbed me by the back of my dress and tossed me to the ground. I slid across the slick marble floor and crashed into the baseboard of a nearby wall.

"Damn!" The twins said in unison.

Beef then backhanded me dead smack in my mouth. "Go change into that maid's outfit."

"You gone get yours," I said, grabbing the shopping bag.

The second floor was as lavishly decorated as the first. I wondered into the master bedroom. *Damn...this is big.* The taupe-painted walls gave the expansive room a cozy feel. I ran my gloved hand over the brown satin comforter that adorned the king-sized bed, looking up at the tray ceilings. Two oak nightstands hugged each side of the bed and a coordinating dresser was situated on the opposing wall. *Wow!* I entered the master bath. There was a Jacuzzi tub, a separate shower that was tiled from floor to ceiling, his and her granite vanities and slate flooring. I touched everything. The grandness of the home reminded me of my grandparent's house.

I reached to touch one of the decorative towels on display in the bathroom just as the doorbell rang again.

"Shut the fuck up." I heard Beef say to Pop and the twins, who were talking and laughing loud as hell.

"Y'all drive a Suburban over here?" Pop asked the twins.

"We rollin' in a Charger."

"Who the fuck is it?"

"The Grim Reaper, motherfucker!"

Hearing the ruckus, I got down on my hands and knees and crawled to the top of the staircase—peering down into the foyer.

Two more niggas, dressed in all black and wearing ski masks, came busting through the front door with AK 47's. "Don't no-fuckin'-body move."

Oh, shit!

"Get down and put your hands behind your head," the gunmen ordered Pop and the twins. They all complied. "Y'all niggas like robbin' people? Huh?" One of the gunmen hit Pop in the back of his head with the butt of his gun.

"Man, I ain't robbed nobody."

"Did I ask you to speak?" He hit him again. "You and your partner-in-crime ain't nothin' but two pussies...two coward-ass stick-up kids." He served the one twin with the same treatment. "But y'all fucked with the wrong one."

"Nigga we don't even know you," Pop said.

"That pregnant lady y'all robbed outside of Christiana Mall was my baby moms, Mother fucker."

"We ain't robbed no bitch."

"Shut the fuck up."

"Please!" One of the twins begged as fluids drained from his body. He had been scared shitless. "I ain't got nothin' to do with y'all beef."

"Yeah, man. He 'bout to leave for college," Beef added.

"For real? Where?" The gunmen in control engaged the twins in a conversation while debating on whether or not to keep them alive or leave them for dead.

"Georgia Tech."

"Oh...so you goin to the A?"

"Yes, Sir, I got athletic scholarships. I'm gone lead'em to another championship."

"What positions you play?"

"Running back...."

"Well...I'm sure y'all would have had a bright future...even a chance at the NFL." The gunman smirked.

"Come on, man. Just let us go," the twin made one last plea for their lives. "My brother won't get into no more shit. I promise."

"That's why you gotta watch the company you keep," the gunman said as he shot each of them...the twins, and Pop one by one...execution style. I looked for Beef but it was like his big ass disappeared in thin air.

* * *

I was blinded by the bright light coming towards me, seeing bits and pieces of my life flash before me. It seemed like I had done more bad than good—the good being me giving birth to my kids. It was the happiest day of my life. I remembered counting all of their tiny fingers and toes to make sure that they were all there and that there weren't any extra. On those days, I had promised to be the best mother I could be to them. It was a promise I had repeatedly broken.

My mind then drifted back to my childhood and settled on thoughts of Tallie—a woman that my parents had hired for a brief time to be mine and my sibling's nanny. She was the only black person to ever step foot inside our house. She was Haitian and had come to the United States like many immigrants—in search of a better life. How she ended up in Delaware was beyond me. I liked Tallie and had spent more time with her than I ever recalled spending with my mother. "By the grace of God chill...you ain't killed ya'self yet," she would say in a thick Caribbean accent every time I took a fall from my bike and scrapped my knees and elbows. She was always there when my mother wasn't.

The light was getting brighter and brighter. And then it was dark—just a passing car.

Dazed and confused, I had walked down the long driveway and wondered barefoot into the street. The gunmen were long gone. They had come to the house for one reason only—to kill the twins, Pop and anyone else in their presence. But, by the grace of God, Beef vanished and they had left me alive.

Asha

Chapter 16

Ki-Ki and I watched as Heedy crept out of Shonni's unit.

"I know she ain't fuckin' that young ass boy," Ki-Ki said, shaking her head and using a hand towel to swat away the summer's bothersome mosquitoes.

"She'll do anything for a designer 'fit."

"She a label whore tho."

Wonder what kind of whore that makes me, I thought. "I'mma go see what's up. I'll talk to you later," I said, putting the thought behind me.

"A'ight...let me know what you find out. I'mma take my ass in the house before these mosquitoes fuck up my legs...be walkin' around here lookin' like Dream. They attacked her real good."

"I told her to get some repellant spray, but she doesn't listen," I said, making my way across the street to Shonni's. The stress that had masked her face following Nic's death had disappeared. She answered the door wearing a smile, which meant she was back in the game—getting money.

"You fuckin' Heedy?" I asked, following her down the hallway of her unit and into her second bedroom turned walk-in closet.

"Hell no! Although his young ass is lookin' good these days and he's paid," she said as she shuffled through a rack of clothes. "He's puttin' me on…three grand. All I gotta do is entertain one of Man-Man's connects."

Getting mixed up with Man-Man was like doing business with the devil. He didn't give a fuck about a nigga's or a broad's soul—only what they could do for him. While he surrounded himself with young niggas like Heedy who were loyal to him, he was loyal to no one. Why she didn't realize that, I had no idea. He just kicked her ass under the curb and now she fuckin' with his people's. She saw what he did to Cream in broad daylight.

"Entertain, huh?"

"You know the business. Plus, bitch, I'm mad at you. Who the hell was that who scooped you up the other night in that Bentley? Don't give me that he's-just-a-friend shit either."

There was a large oval ottoman in the middle of Shonni's closet floor with a stack of magazines resting on it. I moved them to the side and took a seat, picking up the latest issue of Bout that Life' that was on the top of the stack—the Bachelor Baller's edition. It featured twenty-five single men; entrepreneurs, athletes, business men, activists and entertainers. They were men who would never be interested in a woman like me; at least for no longer than one night of pleasure.

"Bitch, don't act like you didn't hear me."

"He *is* just a friend."

"Umm-hmm."

"Really," I said, stuffing the magazine in my purse to scan through later. "He wants to help me turn my life around."

The skeptical look on Shonni's face was the reason why I had thought twice about telling her about Blair. "The shit sounds good, but girl…you can't depend on these niggas. You still gotta stay on your hustle 'cause one minute they're there and the next they're not." Shonni was referring to her own situation but in essence, she was right—which is why I didn't immediately stop tricking.

* * *

The trick's name was Peter of course, I didn't ask. He willingly told me. He was a real-life forty-year-old virgin and like a hormonal teenage boy with a giddy expression on his face, he slid his pants down in anticipation of his first piece of ass. Peter was white with a beer belly. He wore bifocals and his hair was thinning. I stared. *That comb over is a hot ass mess.*

He looked like the serial killer in the movie The Lovely Bones but heavier. He could also be described as the quintessential geek—the guy in high school that got his lunch money taken from him by a bully. *Especially with them Velcro-fastened kicks on.* I shook my head.

Pete had picked me up from off of the Ave. in his mother's grey Taurus station wagon. Every inch of the car, except for the front seat, was packed high with flea-market finds, old newspapers, bags stuffed with clothing from the Goodwill and Salvation Army, tissue paper, can goods and fast-food sacks with uneaten leftovers. Pete, revealed that his mother was a hoarder and that their house looked even worse. Her obsession grew after the death of her husband, his father. He chose to stay with her instead of venturing out into the world. His unselfishness had cost him a life of his own. I felt sorry for him. As I suppose Blair felt for me.

I had decided not to take him up on his offer to help me get "off the streets." *Nigga was talkin' like I was a junky or somethin.' Shit I slowed down on my perc and xannie addiction. Too much shit was happening for me to think about getting high.* And it was hard for me to believe that a man truly wanted to help me without any strings attached and I refused to accept help from a man who pitied me. *I'm nobody's fuckin' charity case.* And as Shonni said, niggas couldn't be depended on. *Too bad I'm not a gold-digger or I'd take him for everything he's worth,* I thought, knowing that deep down I wasn't the conniving-manipulating type.

I lifted my dress over my head as normal and exposed my breasts to Pete. He had already forked over $175 for my Services. His eyes widened like he had seen a ghost and he began to salivate like a starving dog. He walked towards me with his sweaty hands stretched out, ready to palm my tits.

"Stop!"

"Huh?"

"I can't." I reached for my dress on the floor and quickly slipped it back on.

Pete had a confused look on his face. "But, I paid you."

"Here." I handed him the dingy and crunched up bills that he had given me earlier. This is the first time I ever paid a trick back. *There's always a first for everything.*

"Are you serious?" Pete asked, sinking down onto the bed.

"It's not you, it's me," I said, like I was breaking up with a longtime boyfriend.

"Yeah, right," Pete sulked. "I can't even pay a prostitute to sleep with me," he said, sounding suicidal.

No longer could I do it—sell myself short. Whether I could depend on Blair or not, I had to give myself a chance to possibly be all of the things that Lynn wasn't—a productive member of society, someday a wife and most importantly…a loving mother. Whoever Blair was, I was going to trust him even if the role of the dice didn't land in my favor.

"I'm not a prostitute…well…not anymore," I told him, saying it with definiteness and the hope that I would never have to turn another trick for the rest of my life.

* * *

"Girl', you got more people lookin' for you than the FBI got lookin' for Isis." Ki-Ki met me walking from The Budget where I had left Pete to wallow in his misery alone.

She was on her way to Liquor Store to play Ms. Vett's numbers for Wednesday night's Lotto drawing. The jackpot was up to ninety-million dollars and she swore that if she won, she'd tear down the projects homes and rebuild a community of affordable condominiums with a grocery store, beauty salon, retail stores and restaurants below—as the many "live, work and play" residential projects that were being developed in cities across the country. The difference being that Ms. Vett would allow all of the residents that lived in projects to also reside in the

149

condominiums instead of leaving them displaced. It was her take on gentrification.

"Damn," I said. "Who's lookin' for me now?"

"Some white man."

"White man?"

"Yep."

"Fuck...okay."

"Be careful and don't end up on the back of a milk carton," warned Ki-Ki.

Parked in front of my unit was a dark blue charger with tinted windows. If not for the multiple antennas on the vehicle, I would have thought that it was just another cop car copped by a nigga in the hood from a police auction. But, it was an unmarked police cruiser. I started to sweat and imagine the worst—that they thought I had killed Cream or even Dameon for that matter; there had been no sign of him on the streets since I had stun-gunned his ass unconscious. *So I thought he was unconscious. I'm goin' to prison...for murder.* I started to panic but quickly calmed my ass down. After all, I was still a prostitute. *Former prostitute,* I reminded myself. *Who knows the charges they might be tryin' to bring up on me? Then again this might be another dirty cop lookin' for a favor.*

As I proceeded to my unit, the car door to the cruiser opened and an old white man resembling Mr. Perdue stepped out. *His ass is too old to be on the force,* I thought, thinking that I could make a run for it and actually get away.

I walked up the concrete sidewalk leading to my front door, pretending not to see the plain-clothed officer.

"Excuse me," he said footsteps behind me. He was quick for an old man.

. "Can I help you?" I turned to face him.

"Are you Asha Thomas?"

Shit. I could lie and buy some time or tell the truth and get some time. "Who's askin'?"

He extended his hand. "I'm Detective Sam West."

"What you want with me?"

"I was wondering if you had a few minutes to talk."

With each question, I got more defensive. "Talk about what?"

"Your mother and father"

During the initial investigation of their murder, a week didn't go by without Lynn receiving a phone call or a visit from the detectives working the homicide. In time, the visits stopped and so did the calls. It had been a while since we had been contacted about their case and over the years, I had stopped believing that their killer's identity would ever be discovered. I missed them and I did want justice for them.

"My parents?"

"Yes. I'm with WPD's Cold Case Unit and have been assigned to your parents' case. Can we go inside? Or, if you feel comfortable, we can just talk in my car."

"We can talk in the cruiser."

Out of courtesy, the detective opened the passenger-side door for me. "Leave it open," I said as he gestured to close it.

"Ms. Thomas," he began. "After reviewing this case, I've come across some disturbing information."

"What kind of information?"

Her file seems to be missing…the ballistic report and some pictures taken of the scene which leads me to believe that the detectives handling this case were involved in a some kind of cover up.

The coroner's report showed that shortly before the deaths, my mother had engaged in sexual intercourse. However, with her being married to my father, he ruled out that she had been raped. Still, there were bruises on the insides of her thighs and on her wrists from her attacker pinning her down. I imagined her kicking and screaming—fighting for her life. After a failed attempt to strangle her, he shot her twice in the abdomen. She bled to death. He said my father was found outside the car shot in the head.

"It's going to take some more investigating on my part to pinpoint the trigger man, but I just wanted to let you know that I am one-hundred percent dedicated to finding your parent's killer and bringing him down...I promise."

He went on to ask me a few questions about the last time I saw my parents alive.

Shonni

Chapter 17

Like a K-9 trained to sniff out narcotics, I could smell a stank-nasty attitude on a bitch from a mile away—which was exactly what I smelled when I walked into Jael's; along with the usual mixture of chemicals and the scent of hot irons. Jael was in the middle of rehashing the latest episode of Love and Hip Hop: Atlanta to the salon's stylists and afternoon patrons but as soon as I made my presence known, the conversation stopped and the whispers started.

"Hey, y'all."

"Hey, snow girl Shonni," Jael was slow to speak.

"What is wrong with everybody up in here?" I asked, wasting no time to clear the air.

"Yeah...that's her friend," I heard Jella—the newest addition to the crew. "We met her when Asha and I had hit the salon up." she whispered in the ear of another Jael's' stylist.

"Who the fuck is *her*?" I asked. "Let's cut to the chase," I said, ready to *cut* the first bitch who stepped

154

to me with the box *cutter* in my purse—including Jael's ass. "I don't have to be here if it's a problem. I can take my money to Kristoff like I been doing sweetness." I sneered at Jella. She frowned and rolled her eyes, but didn't say shit. *That's what I thought.*

Tink appeared from the back of the salon looking malnourished and like she hadn't slept in days. She was in desperate need of a trip to Hometown Buffet and a 5-Hour Energy Drink. Her puffy eyes were encased in dark circles, which—on her light skin—appeared to be two black eyes and her hair was unkempt. And that was poor marketing and advertising for a bitch who was a stylist. *She gone have to do somethin' about that new growth.*

"How's your triflin' ass friend, Asha?" She asked, taking me by surprise. *Fuck me,* I thought, figuring out the reason for the built-up tension in the salon. *Asha must have fucked her man.*

"She's wrong for what she did…as long as Tink's been doin' her hair," Jael contributed his two cents.

"That's some foul shit to do," Jella finally found the nerve to speak up. "I called Tink ASAP when I spotted Asha in the front seat of Dameon's car."

"I'm not Asha. So, any beef you got with her then you need to take it up with her. That's how a grown ass woman would handle the situation," I told Tink.

"You're right," she said, leaving the matter alone and moving on to the next. "What you want done to today?" She asked, gesturing for me to take a seat in her chair. *She must think I'm crazy.* There was no way I was letting her up in my head with a pair of scissors and a hot ass flat iron nearby. *She ain't about to fuck my shit up. And I ain't even the one who fucked her man.*

"I'm cool," I said, backing out the door and I decided to place a call to the young girl that sold, *Barbie Extensions* bundles of hair. I would have to call upon Kristoff after all.

In route to the hair spot, I decided to stop by the liquor store first to get Kim to thread my eyebrows. A strung-out group of crack-heads were out in front of the store circling the dope boys like a pack of vultures. *Damn.* That new shit that Heedy had told me about called Power had hit the streets—illegal transactions were being made left and right. Man-Man had switched briefcases—cash in one and product in the other—with his Haitian connect the night before and let the drug loose. *Man-Man killin' the game with that Power. It must be some strong shit.* The drug was selling faster than the iPhone 7 I scanned the growing drug-addicted crowd of mothers, fathers, daughters, sons, aunts and uncles and like a hot flash, a wave of sadness came over me as I thought about the devastation that a drug addiction caused. It tore families apart and ruined communities, but who was to blame—the fiend for using drugs or the dealer for selling them?

Entertaining Man-Man's connect was the extent of my involvement in the dope game. He was still in town looking to have a good time, which is where I came into play. My instructions were to seduce him and keep him coming back for more of me and to do business with Man-Man—making my contribution to the drug infestation in the projects and surrounding hoods larger than I thought. I couldn't help but to wonder if Manson knew it was me doing this for him.

I had made it clear to Heedy that this was a one-time deal. I wanted to make my entry into the dope game quick and easy. *Get in and get out,* I told myself—hoping that the three grand Man-Man gave Heedy to give me would hold me over until I recruited another team of sponsors. The words of advice that Ms. Vett had given me about "having my own" had went in one ear and out the other as well as the idea of picking up my kids.

Walking towards the store, I was met by a middle-aged black woman with a stack of pamphlets in her hand. She handed me one. It detailed a program sponsored by a non-profit organization called *Taking back the you.*

"I ain't no crack head," I said, tossing the pamphlet to the ground.

"You ain't gotta be a crack head. It's a program for addicts, drug dealers, prostitutes and anyone else who wants to turn their life around," she preached.

"Thanks, but no thanks." I left her standing there.

"I just got a big shipment of Effin Vodka," he said.

"I'm not buying' liquor today. I came to see Kim."

"Oh...Kim in back...go ahead," he said, allowing me behind the curtain that separated the front of the store from the back.

"What up, girl?" Kim asked. She was fluent in English, Japanese and Chinese.

"Not shit...need my eyebrows done. What you been up too?"

"Just working makin' that paper."

"You know it."

"You ready?"

"Yep," I said, preparing myself for the winces of pain that came with getting a thread job. *No pain, no gain.*

* * *

The jet black freshly dyed Brazilian stretched down my back. My bangs were cut with precision and hung perfectly to the tip of my brow line. Kristoff had hooked my hair up. I was getting my sexy Minaj look on for Man-Man's connect. Black hair was a good look for me. *I might just dye my own hair black. If looks could kill I would be killin' the game.* The short red dress hugging my hips matched my lipstick and the "girls" were propped high on my chest like two water-filled balloons. They bounced in unison with every step I took down the carpeted hall of the spacious Dupont Hotel. I had just walked through the garden conservatory. It was the perfect setting for a spring wedding. I was never one of those little girls who day dreamed about her wedding day or even considered saying "I do". I fantasized about scheming niggas and getting what I could get from them. But, I often wondered if my outlook on life, love and marriage would have been different if my father hadn't checked out on my mother.

As I stood in front of the double doors of Presidential Suite, the doors to the suite behind me opened. I turned to see who was vacating the room and came face-to-face with a pleasant surprise—a finger-licking fine ass nigga. *Damn! He can get it.* Beneath the suit and tie he had on was the aura of a hustler—a mad man, which made him even more irresistible. He smiled but didn't give me the attention I was looking for. Nor did I notice the beef-head nigga that had tailed him out of the hotel room. They headed down the hall. *Wonder who the fuck that was?*

Returning my attention back to the suite in front of me, I ran my tongue over my teeth to lick away any smudges of stray lipstick and knocked on the double doors with force. My eyes widened. The biggest Haitian man that I had ever seen in my life answered.

159

This nigga got to be in the Guinness Word Book of Records for being the biggest man alive. He was the connects bodyguard and must have been expecting me because he let me in without asking me my name, but I didn't get very far before he frisked me down and rummaged through my purse. *Thank goodness I switched purses.* He seated me in the formal living room of the suite and disappeared. I scanned the room, awed by the ceiling-to-floor fish tank set-up against one of the walls. My attention was quickly diverted to the bar in the corner of the room. Never missing an opportunity to fix myself a drink, I strolled over—choosing the top-shelf vodka. *Just what I needed.*

"I see you're enjoying yourself," The Connect said in seemingly perfect English, walking into my presence.... I gulped down the last of the vodka in my glass. *I'mma need another drink for this.*

"I like your hair…reminds me of a China doll," he said, fixing himself a drink and me another.

"Thank, you." I slithered towards him. *Game time.* "What's your name?" I asked.

"Guy," he said, already enthralled in my cleavage.

"Is that your real name?"

He laughed. "Yes, it's pronounced GEE.

"Like ME-huh"

"What's your name?" He asked.

"Shon…" I said.

"Shon. You're a beautiful black woman. I'm going to have to thank Manson for being so kind to me."

"Let me show you how kind I can be." I removed a cube of ice from my glass and rubbed it all over my chest. He watched as the ice chilled my skin, causing my nipples to harden. "Lead the way," I said and smiled following him to the suite's master bedroom.

Carly

Chapter 18

With extra precaution, I tiptoed to the door. Every second that I was awake—from the moment that I had hitched a ride from the Greenville mansion back to South Bridge—I sensed that someone was watching me. Like a fugitive on the run, I was constantly looking over my shoulders and hoping that the masked murderers hadn't regretted leaving me alive or that the police weren't on my trail. Whoever was at the door wouldn't go away. They kept knocking, determined for me to answer.

"What the hell?"

Dream stood in front of me wearing a surgical mask. "Zinka ain't no joke…killin' Brazilians left and right. I can't take no chances. My kids won't have anybody if somethin' happens to me," she explained. "And you need some milk." She looked my mosquito-bitten body up and down. I ignored her comment and let her in.

Over the last couple of weeks, everybody in the projects had seen me come and go with Beef and Pop. And when the news of the murders hit the airwaves, she was the first to warn me that niggas had been snitching.

"Y'all bitches stay in some shit.

"Can you please refrain from disrespecting me in my own home?" I asked Dream, glancing at Synda asleep on the couch.

"No," she said bluntly. "If y'all respected y'all's selves than y'all would get respect."

"Anyways," Dream continued. "The block is hot. Undercover cops are swarmin' around here askin' questions."

"Really?"

"Really."

"Who's talkin'?"

"Big-mouth Dosha. She done told the cops all your little business...how you had been hangin' tough with Pop...she actin' like them niggas that be snitchin' on The First 48 for a cigarette and a soda...weak asses."

"Damn-it-to-hell."

"I guess when you fuck as much as you fuck you bound to get *fucked*," Dream slid in another insult. "I'm surprised the police ain't came knockin' on your door yet. Oh..." She pointed to the television. "Turn up the volume."

An older black man appeared on the screen. His eyes were red with grief. He was the twins' uncle and served as their family's spokesperson. "My sister was raisin' her boys right," he said into the camera. "They were respectful…made good grades and stayed out of trouble. We just ask that you keep our family in your thoughts and prayers."

The media had dubbed the murders of Pop and the twins as *The Greenville Murders*. Such a tragedy taking place in the exclusive suburb of the city had attracted outside attention. News coverage of the twins' mother falling to the ground and fainting at the roped-and-taped off murder scene had been broadcast on all of the local and national news stations. She had been a single mother of three- *And now one.* During the day, she attended nursing school. And at night, she worked the third-shift at a nursing home as a nurse's aide. She was making the sacrifices a mother made when she wanted a better life for herself and her children—the media reported.

The twins were highly courted by Division Ivy League schools and as they said, had signed to play football at the Georgia Tech. They were well on their way to achieving a higher education and making their dreams of playing in the NFL come true.

They were lying because only one of them had made it into college the other was robbing knocked up chicks with Pop.

"That's a damn shame," Dream said.

Pop was an afterthought in the news story as if his life was of lesser value than the twins because of his long rap sheet. I remembered the scroll tattoo on Pop back that paid homage to all of his slain friends and family members. *You live by the gun; you die by the gun.* Pop's mother defended her son by saying that the loss of his life was just as devastating as the deaths of the twins. The story did feature seconds of Pop's family and friends gathered at a vigil and wearing airbrushed t-shirts that read R.I.P. Pop.

"Niggas quick to get some t-shirts made," Dream commented.

The reporter covering the story summed up his report. "The deaths of the Hawkins appear to be an unfortunate event of the young men being in the wrong place at the wrong time." He looked down at the piece of paper in his hands. "In lieu of flowers, the family is asking that donations be made at Bank of America where a scholarship fund has been set up in honor of the brothers. They money will go to help deserving young students attend college...something the Hawkins had hoped of doing. I'm Gavun Miles reporting for Action News Channel 6."

The anchor in the news studio added to the end of the coverage. "The family of the Hawkins Boys are offering a $15,000 reward to anyone who has any information that will help aid the police in their

165

investigation. Please call Crime Stoppers with any tips leading to the arrest of the killer or killers." With ease, she moved on to a feel-good story about a cat being rescued out of a tree by firefighters.

"What you gone do?" Dream turned to me and asked.

The worst some would think, I thought. "Nothin'."

I walked over to Ms. Vett's to see if she heard from her nephew beef.

"You know Dosha been snitchin' on you." She said as soon as I walked in.

"I know. Dream already told me."

"So, do you know what went down? Were you with them? Do you know who did it?" She bombarded me with questions that she already knew the answers to.

I felt like I was on the stand in a courtroom, open to interrogation.

"No." I had already decided to take what I knew to the grave. No one, including Dream, knew the extent of my involvement in the murders and I wanted to keep it that way—between me, God, the deceased and the gunmen.

"No?" she repeated.

"No…I don't know what went down. I wasn't with them and I don't know who did it."

"You keep it that way. By the way Beef is fine." she added.

* * *

In the middle of the night, I woke up drenched in sweat. I willed myself to sit up in the bed. My gown was damp and clung to my body. The sight of Cream, Pop and the twins taking their last breaths had been haunting me in my dreams and taking a toll on me physically and mentally. And the guilt I felt for not reporting my eye witness account of the murders to the police was making matters worse.

On top of the nightmares and night sweats, I wasn't feeling any better than I was on the day of the murders and had tried every over-the-counter medication and home remedy to rid my body the aches, pains and nauseating feeling in the pit of my stomach. Nothing was working. Along with it all, I had been ambushed by blood-sucking mosquitoes who left small red bite marks over my body.

Synda touched my forehead with the back of her tiny hand as she had seen me do many times before when she was sick. "Carly, you're burning up," she said so matter-of-factly. I didn't have the strength to reprimand her for calling me Carly so I let it slide. *For now...*

"You as red as when Asha hit you." I frowned and turned my nose up at her. *She didn't have to say all that.* "You want me to dial 911 like you showed me?" She asked.

"Mommy don't need 911." She looked at me with an expression that told me she thought otherwise. I finally made an appointment at the Henrietta Johnson Health Clinic.

Asha

Chapter 19

All of my senses were aroused as Blair maneuvered the car from street to street. He knew the city better than he had initially led me to believe the day he stopped and asked me for directions. It was a ploy, but I didn't know for what. And in that particular moment, I didn't care.

As we rode, Bryson Tiller's voice filtered from the car's speakers. The scent of Blair's cologne circulated throughout the car along with the beats of the song and the sight of him steering the car with one arm and moving his head to the beat made my vagina jump—it never jumped for the tricks I tricked with. It remained dormant but still got the job done.

I pinched myself to make sure that the moment was real and that it wasn't all a dream because dreams just didn't come true where I was from. Nor did it seem like prayers were answered—I could testify to that. And there sure as hell weren't any fairytale endings amidst the chaos and destruction that wade in the streets. There was just more of the same ol' shit—nigga's trying to get by...by any means necessary.

Ouch! I pinched myself a little bit too hard. I wasn't dreaming. Instead of sending someone to contact me about my decision to "stay at the bottom or rise to the top" as he had put it, Blair pleasantly surprised me himself. *Damn, he could have caught a bitch at a better time,* I thought, looking down at my I-ain't-leaving-the-house-today-for-shit attire when he knocked on my unit door. I was wearing a pair leggings and white wife beater. Blair was back in street mode—out of the Wall street suit and tie that he was perfectly tailored in the last time I saw him inside his Presidential Suite out at the Gaylord hotel. I didn't know what to think of his Clark Kent-Superman mystique. Only that it had me intrigued.

Standing in my doorway, he had on a pair of True Religion rugged jeans, a gray polo shirt with a crisp white-tee underneath and the latest, red patent Christian Louboutin studded sneaks. He was giving Kanye some competition for his best-dressed title in the game.

"Are you going to invite me in?"

"My bad." I had gotten caught up.

"You look good."

"Ha-ha. You got jokes," I said, letting him in.

170

"Nah. I'm just sayin'…you look good when you look regular…not how you look when you're out there on your hustle."

"Thanks…I guess."

He meant to say I looked good minus the make-up, spandex dress, clear plastic stripper shoes and weave. Earlier, I had unstitched my sew-in, washed and roller set my natural hair. It hung softly to my shoulders. I didn't have any extra money to go to the salon—not that I would ever be going back to Jael. Word on the street was that Tink was looking for me. *She ain't lookin' too damn hard…everybody else seems to find me.* I wasn't the one she needed to be looking for though; Dameon was still missing. The longer he was incognito, the more relieved I felt—doubting that me taserin' his ass had killed him. I was sure the housekeepers at The Courtyard would have found his decaying body by now.

Blair eyed my unit, from ceiling-to-floor and wall-to-wall, taking the sight of my rented furniture. I wasn't into fucking niggas for couches. I left that up to Shonni. I did what I did…to get by.

"You read that yet?"

"What?"

"That issue of *Bout that life*?" Blair pointed to the magazine that I had copped from Shonni. It was lying on my glass coffee table.

"No…not yet."

He quickly changed the subject to the reason why he was there. "You made your decision yet?"

"Yeah, I decided."

"What you gone do?"

"I'mma rise to the top." *Whateva the hell that entails.*

Blair pulled me in close to him and gripped my tiny waist. "I want nothin' but the best for you Asha Thomas. Come with me somewhere."

"Where?"

"You'll see."

* * *

The car stopped. *I know the hell we ain't.* But, we were—parked in front of the Salvation Army. *This ain't the mall.* Broads that I knew who dated drug dealers, in which I suspected Blair was—that or a pimp—had always bragged about going on thousand-dollar shopping sprees, trips to the nail salon and eating steak and lobster every day. I frowned. *This nigga got me at the homeless shelter.*

"Ummm…did we make a wrong turn?"

"No." Blair chuckled.

"Well, I'm not homeless."

"I know and this isn't just a homeless shelter. They offer help to everyone."

"I'm not a drug addict or an alcoholic either."

"I hope not."

I playfully punched Blair in the arm. "Why are we here?"

"There's somebody that I want you to meet…a dear friend of mine."

He got out of the car and walked over to open my door for me. Stubbornly, I got out. On the outside, the building looked like a hangout for junkies. But inside, it was clean and bright—as sterile as an operating room. Blair was bombarded by its' inhabitants—giving him pats on the back and dap. Some of them were familiar faces that I'd seen from around the way. I nodded hello and smiled as Blair grabbed my hand and led me down a hall of offices. We came to a halt in front of a glass door with stenciling that read Take your life Back INTAKE OFFICE.

An older black woman looked up from her desk. She was tall and slender—beautiful once upon a time but behind her smile was a story of struggle and survival.

"Blair!" She hugged and kissed him on the cheek. "I've got everything under control."

"I know you do. I'm just stopping by to introduce you to the new lady in my life. This is Asha. And Asha, this is Pam."

"Nice to meet you," we both exchanged pleasantries.

"I'm going to the back and holla at some of the fellows. I'll leave you two ladies to get acquainted."

I scanned her office. On the wall behind her desk was a framed diploma that she had received for graduating from the program. Also tacked to the wall were several inspirational sayings and scriptures. I read the one that caught my eye. *If you keep doing what you're doing...you'll keep getting what you're getting.*

"So, tell me about yourself," she said.

"Tell me about yourself?" I responded, upset that Blair had clearly drug me down to the mission for some apparent therapy session. I was a prostitute who decided to stop prostituting. To me, my problem was solved. But, there were always deeper reasons for our behavior.

"Okay," she laughed. "You remind me so much of myself...stubborn," she said before going on. "For starters, I'm a recovering crack addict. I almost lost my life several times, but the last time I was truly on the brink of death. I was attacked by one of my dealer's girlfriends. She thought I was after her man, but I was just trying to suck his dick so that I could get high. I was taken to the hospital, but they didn't do shit but give me some Tylenol and sent my ass on my merry little way. But, my spleen was ruptured. I thought I had taken my last breath on top of a cardboard box in an alleyway where I used to get high and turn tricks along with other crack-heads. But, when I thought my life was over...the man above..."

She pointed to the sky. "He saved me. Until this day, I don't know who but somebody took me to get some medical attention somewhere. I must have passed out. All I remember is waking up on a Greyhound bus headed here to Delaware. There was some cash and a note in an envelope instructing me to take a taxi to an address that was written down on the note. The taxi dropped me off right here at the mission. God saved my life and the Take your life Back program changed it."

My eyes watered. Pam handed me a Kleenex. "That's deep."

"Honey, everybody has a story...only a few live to have a testimony. I know you're not an addict, but I know Blair didn't bring you here because you were an angel."

"No," I laughed. "Far from it. I'm a...well...I use to turn tricks over on New Castle Avenue.

"How did you get into prostitution?" Pam asked me without condemnation in her voice.

"My aunt was a prostitute and so was my cousins. I guess you can say whorin' runs in my family."

"Children will do as they see."

"You have any children?" I asked Pam.

"I have a daughter named Clarissa. She's in prison...locked away for life over a nigga. I haven't seen her in years, but we write back-and-forth. She's doing good…as good as one can be doing behind bars. But, tell me more about your mother."

"Her name was Linda she was murdered along with my father. So at the old age of twelve I went to go live with my Aunt Lynsey, my fathers' sister. My Aunt whored everywhere…on the corner, in the back of cars, down at The Days Inn, dirty-needle-infested alleys and anywhere in between…the same places I grew up turning tricks. But, the worst was when she would bring tricks home with her. I hated her for a lot of things but for that the most. Our homes are supposed to be our safe havens…our sanctuaries…the place we go to escape the streets. I've never turned a trick inside my house…not one."

"Where's your Aunt now?"

"Dead."

"I'm sorry to hear that."

"I wish I was. The life she lived…I can't even say she's in a better place."

"What happened? If you don't mind me asking."

The last time I saw Lynn alive, she was reapplying her lipstick and tussling with her thick dusty-brown hair. She had just returned to the Ave. from seeing a trick named Bill. I remembered seeing his name stitched into the fabric of his oil-stained shirt when he approached us. I guessed that he was a mechanic, just getting off of work and trying to get some different pussy before he headed home to the same ol' pussy—

as was the case with many of the tricks that sought our services.

A Chrysler 300 rolled up to the Ave. The trick behind the wheel put the car in park and leaned across the front seat, calling out to us through the passenger side window.

"Which one of you hoe's available?"

"I am," I said, starting to walk towards him. Before I could take another step, Lynn tugged at my wrist. "Let me take this one."

"Huh?"

"You can get the next one."

"I haven't made half the money you've made today. You're a greedy whore," I said to her.

Pam handed me another Kleenex as I cried, reliving the day and recalling the last words that I said to my Aunt.

"Asha, I don't have time to argue with your ass right now but your ass is grass. You fuck like a grown woman, but I'm gone whoop you like the child you are when I get back."

I remember just rolling my eyes at her as she reached for the car's door handle. She hopped in. The next time I saw her was at the morgue.

"Asha," Pam said my name in a low whisper. "Did you ever stop to think that your aunt sensed that this man was dangerous? And although you never believed that she was meant to be a mother…that she was put on this earth to protect you in that one moment in time?"

Shonni

Chapter 20

The $3,000 that I had earned from "entertaining" Man-Man's connect was burning a hole in my Gucci handbag. The purse itself had cost me $2,900 so $3,000 was pennies compared to the money I had trickling in each month from Nic, Dale, Manson and Neil—before everything went haywire. And because I hadn't rounded up another team of sponsors yet, I had to watch how I handled what little I had.

I used my right hand to pry the newest arrival at the Louis Vuitton store out of my left one and reluctantly handed the handbag back to Lori—the store associate. We were on a first name basis being that I had visited the store so many times over the years that my footprints were worn into the floor of the luxury boutique.

"You sure, girl?" Lori asked. "You know you are always the first to rock the new-new."

I threw my head back in despair, feeling defeated. "Yeah, I'm sure," I said and sulked out of the store. I had also put back a pair of Via Spiga sandals at Nordstroms, leaving the mall as I have never left it before—emptied handed.

Fuck this! I swerved my car in the direction of Shop Rite—not for groceries but to shop for sponsors.

Damn. It's a slow day. I had made my way up-and-down each aisle of the store twice and hadn't run into any possible prospects. *Maybe I spoke too soon*, I thought as I spotted a nigga heading down the produce aisle.

I threw a few items in my cart as if I was really grocery shopping and preceded in his direction. I inched the cart down the aisle, scanning him from head-to-toe. *Okay...nice fade...smooth chocolate skin...cute smile...small gap but his teeth are still on point...blue tie...white button-up...black belt with nickel buckle...black slacks to match...and... ummm...NO. Seriously?* If there was one thing I couldn't stand, it was a nigga with no shoe game. I shook my head in disappointment as I stared at the tips of his shoes. They were severely scuffed—on shoe life support. *If he can't afford a three-dollar bottle of black shoe polish, then I know he can't afford me.* I pushed my cart right past him without a hey, hi, hello or how you doing?

Before I could make it to the end of the aisle, a loud beeping sound came over the store's intercom.

"Attention shoppers, if you are the owner of a red Infiniti…you're being towed."

I broke out in a gold-medal sprint, breaking the heel on my left shoe. *Damn it!* I hobbled out the store on the strength of one leg where I saw my car being lifted onto the back of a tow truck.

"What the hell are you doin'?" I yelled at the nigga operating the tow truck. "I wasn't even parked illegally."

"I know."

"You know? Then why the hell are you towin' my shit?"

"Let me introduce myself," he said, removing his right hand from a dirt-and-oil-stained glove. "I'm the repo man and the bank sent me to get your *shit*."

"The bank?"

"The bank," he reiterated.

My mouth dropped. "What? My car is paid for. It must be a mistake."

"No mistake and…don't I know you?" He asked.

This is not the time to be tryin' to holla. "No. You don't."

"Yeah…yeah, I do. You're the chick from Lavish. I'm the guy that was sitting at the other end of the bar…the one you ignored after I bought you a drink. I guess you thought I wasn't good enough for you."

"Evidently not." *What the hell he want me to do, apologize?*

"I know I was lookin' rough, but I had just stopped in the club for a drink."

"Can we talk about how I can get my car down from there?" I pointed to the back of the tow-truck bed, ignoring him once again.

"I want to talk to your manager."

"You're talkin' to him."

"Huh?"

"I'm Blake. I'm the CEO and owner of Blake's Repo Company. I'm usually in the office doing paperwork, but I like to get out and get dirty every once in a while." He winked and then I remembered the last words he said to me at the club. *Don't let your eyes fool you.*

To make matters worse, it dawned on me that—while under the hair dryer at Kristoff's about six months earlier—I had glanced over an article in The Delaware Today magazine about Blake's Repo Company being the fastest growing minority-owned company across the state, bringing in profits close to a million dollars in its' three short years in business. Its' headquarters was in Dover, but the company operated in the Tri-State Area. Dwelling on how I had played myself by not giving Blake any play because I thought he was just another nigga struggling to get by would have been a waste of time. *You lose one to get one.* But, I was still a tad bit salty—Blake would have made for a perfect sponsor.

"What I gotta do to get my ride back?"

Blake walked to the cab of the tow truck and grabbed a clip board full of paperwork. "You need to wire Wells Fargo Bank $2,777.32."

To my surprise and obviously, the car was not paid in full as I had thought. *Nic better be glad his ass is already six-feet under.*

"When payment is confirmed," he went on. "I'll put her back down," he said, referring to my car.

Saying so myself, I was the queen seductress and the art of seduction worked on many niggas. But, he looked like he wasn't having it. He didn't become a millionaire by putting pussy before business. I turned my ass around and hobbled back into the store, hoping that I had enough from the $3,000 left to wire the bank their money.

* * *

The car was back in my possession and I was broke because of it. I was wardrobe rich and cash poor; I had nineteen cents inside a $2,900 Gucci handbag. *I didn't have two dimes to rub together.* The stress of being in the red would have driven any weak-minded person to drive their car into the Chesapeake Bay still buckled in. In fact, there had been several people to do so—mostly middle-aged white men who had lost their jobs in the recession. But no matter how fucked up life got, I would never intentionally stop my own heart from beating. And I never fully understood why anybody would, including my own father— regardless of the situation.

There was a period of time when I was younger— before my mother had completely neglected us—in which, she had tried to seek the Lord. For twelve Sundays straight, she drug me to the Pentecostal Church on the corner. I kept count because I knew that her religious run would eventually come to an end. During the majority of the Services, I passed notes back-and-forth with my siblings. Although I could barely recall an entire sermon, I do remember the first words that came out of the preacher's mouth each time he stepped foot in the pulpit. "No matter what happened yesterday, today is a new day in which you have another chance to devote your life to Christ."

I didn't know about the "devoting my life to Christ" part, but I knew that I wouldn't let me being broke today ruin my hustle for tomorrow. I loved my life and I was going to keep living it the way I had grown accustom to being-fabulous, even if I un-intentionally made choices that would eventually led to my own demise.

* * *

Dollar stood guard outside of Manson's trap house as he always did. *Does that nigga even take a piss break?* There was never a time when I had driven by the trap and didn't see Dollar standing at his post. Rain, sleet or snow that nigga was on the job.

"What's up, Dollar?"

"Ain't nothin'. What's good with you, Shonni?" He had a weird look on his face.

"Not too much right now. I need to get at Man-Man."

"You know he hot with you right?"

"It's cool I just need to speak with him-for a minute."

Big Rock Radioed Man-Man on the walkie-talkie in his hand. "Shonni out here," he said. "She cool?"

"Yeah, let her through," Manson radioed back.

Dollar motioned for me to enter through the large steel door and almost immediately, I was hit in the face with a fistful of smoke. *Damn, did a bomb go off in this motherfucker?* I asked myself, choking and trying to cough up the smoke that had seeped down my windpipe and into my lungs. If I hadn't known the difference between weed smoke and smoke from a burning Ki-Ki, I would have stopped, dropped and rolled.

Squinting, to limit the amount of smoke getting into my eyes and holding my breath, I made my way through the trap house. As the heavy fog of smoke began to dissipate, I noticed extracurricular activities taking place throughout the trap house. *This shit is unsanitary,* I thought—stepping over puddles of body fluids and not prepared for what I was about to witness.

He—the nigga that was about to die—had a black pillowcase over his head. His hands were tied behind his back and his wrists were raw and bleeding from the tight hold of the rope. His bare feet were also bound at the ankles. They appeared to be worse off than his bloody wrists. To my eyes, he was unidentifiable. But, I was sure Heedy and Man-Man knew exactly who he was. He was on his knees, begging for his life. His speech was slurred and his voice unrecognizable as if his tongue had been chopped off. But what I could make out of what he was trying to explain was that his girl was the only other person who knew where he kept his stash of money and product. She had set him up.

"Man-up, young nigga!" Man-Man shouted at Heedy. "Kill that schemin' ass nigga…teach these niggas around here a lesson. Nobody steals from me and lives…not even my own got-damn mama." Manson's mother had disappeared a year earlier. *Guess that solves that case.*

Heedy towered over the soon-to-be-deceased, aiming the gun in his trembling sixteen-year-old hand pointblank at the nigga's head. The armpits of his Hollister T-shirt were damp with sweat. He was a boy ordered to do a man's job. *Manson was one cold-blooded nigga.*

"Maybe I should come back," I said, standing in the doorway of Man-Man's office and nervously tapping my right foot.

Man-Man held up his index finger, gesturing for me to stay put and give him a minute while he took care of the business in front of him first. "What the fuck you waitin' on? Waste that nigga," Man-Man continued to egg him on.

I turned my head in the same manner the news often showed bystanders ignoring the cries for help of a person being robbed on a busy street or adults walking past a teenage brawl without uttering a mumbling word. *Fuck. I wasn't tryin' to see a nigga die today,* I thought—hoping that the guilt of not intervening wouldn't eat me alive.

I didn't hear the gunshot, just the trigger being pulled and a loud thud as the dead weight hit the floor. There was a silencer on the gun. A few seconds later, Manson waved me into his office.

"Shonni, Heedy and I were talkin' 'bout you earlier."

"Oh, yeah," I said, stepping over the deceased.

"Yeah. You know I was pissed with your ass but Heedy told me what you did for me. I appreciate it and I forgive you. You got our little connect pussy-whipped already. He wants to see you again, but I told him you said it was a one-time deal. I was just gone stick another freak on him, but you have the best pussy around."

"First-of-fuckin'-all," I rolled my neck and put my hands on my hips. "I ain't no freak and you loved fucking me. I'm just havin' some cash-flow problems right now…gotta do what I gotta do…and I miss you." I added.

"Cool. Here." Manson tossed two G's in my direction with no expressions. "The connect is still in town…go holla at him tonight before he leaves…give him somethin' to think about. Come back for the rest tomorrow."

I didn't get Manson completely back on my team but-my handbag was heavier when I walked out of the trap house than when I walked in, but at one cost—I was now an eye witness to a murder. My conscience was even heavier.

* * *

There was a charcoal-gray Porsche parked in front of Asha's unit. *That hoe is pullin' niggas in Porsche's and Bentleys.* It looked like Asha was piecing together a team of sponsors herself. She had always worked the avenue, slobbing on the knobs of slimy tricks for less than a stack. *Now, those niggas she used to fuckin' are petty.* I suppose I should have been happy for her, but a wave of jealousy hit me as my sponsor game was dwindling down and hers appeared to be looking up.

Ki-Ki was sitting in a lawn chair in front of her unit, eating Barbeque-flavored sunflower seeds and drinking an orange Fanta. "Hey, Ki-Ki," I walked over and spoke. "I see you got on enough Vaseline to grease up an army of ashy niggas."

"Fuck you, Shonni. That's why your shit almost got repo'd." *Damn.* My business had already hit the pavement. "Dosha said that she saw it all. She was comin' out of the liquor store from cashin' her disability check along with her dead mama's social security check too."

"I know she done already told everybody."

"You know it. She knockin' on doors spreadin' your business. You better go beg for my cousin Man-Man to take your ass back. I can put in a word for you." She laughed. To my surprise my oldest son-Sonny came running out of her house.

"Ms. Ki-Ki! Dream pee'd on herself, It's a whole bunch of pee too."

Ki-Ki jumped up, knocking over her can of soda and rushing into her unit, Dream's water had broken.

"Okay...okay...somebody call 911!" Ki-Ki ordered.

"Uggghhh...it shit! It hurts so bad!" Dream screamed.

"It's supposed to hurt ain't it?" Ki-Ki said.

"Get the fuck out my face talking dumb," Dream moaned.

189

They both started bickering as usual.

"We gone have to take her to the hospital." Ki-Ki shouted.

"In whose car?" I asked, knowing that I was the only one around with a vehicle. I frowned at the secretions running down her legs. "She can't get in my car like that."

"Get me some towels." Ki-Ki lowered Dream onto the bathroom floor, removed her panties and spread her legs open. "It looks like I'll be deliverin' this baby."

"Bitch no the fuck you ain't. I'm not having my baby on the bathroom floor! Dream snapped.

"The baby head is right here girl! We gotta do this now!"

Dream palmed her knees and pushed. A few big pushes later, a little boy with a head full of curly hair came gushing out from between her legs.

In the same day, I had witnessed a life being taken out of the world and another welcomed into it—the most horrific moment in life and the most precious. *What a cruel yet tender world?* I thought, holding the baby in my arms.

Carly

Chapter 21

The doctor confirmed what I had secretly suspected. I had been tested and diagnosed all in one day. I wasn't pregnant or sick from the foreign substance that I had been injecting into my lips. My fate was much worse and I suppose I had been in denial for years—not wanting to accept the fact that the red mosquito bites on my body were actually the occurrence of small lesions. And I was still in denial; I went to Walgreens to buy some Benadryl as Ki-Ki had suggested—aware that what I had couldn't be cured especially not with pills. Neither the police nor the gunmen had been following me. It was the shadow of death hovering over me. I had witnessed life taken and now faced my own mortality.

Synda had escaped to the toy section of the store while I roamed the health and beauty aisles. "Mama, can I get this?" She came running towards me with a $6.99 knock-off Barbie. *She would remember to call me mama when she wants somethin'.*

"Sure." I was in no mood to tell her no.

At the counter, the clerk rang the items up.

I spoke, paid and grabbed the plastic bag. With my mind clouded, I didn't even see the army of police officers waiting for me outside of the store with their hands planted on their holsters—ready to aim, shoot and Ki-Ki. *Damn. You would've thought I pulled some Set-It-Off shit. Guess they were followin' me.*

"Carly Felton?" One of the officers approached me.

"Yes?"

"We need you to come with us to the station for questioning regarding the murders of Milton Williams and Taron and Tarin Hawkins."

"Can I call somebody to come and pick up my daughter first?"

"That will be fine, Ms. Felton."

* * *

When the police bum rushed me in front of Walgreens, I tried but couldn't get a hold of Ms. Vett. My only other option was to call Asha. Synda liked her and that night me and Cream was in the car she did take her in. I smiled at Synda, she looked happy. I was in a fucked up situation and I wasn't sure how everything was going to play out. Zoe snatched Symia from Ms. Vett's as soon as she heard the police picked me up; I wasn't shocked. They been wanting to get their hands on her. They claimed she was the only one who was really Creams baby. Synere was out

Brookmont staying with my sister Nola he didn't want anything to do with me...I couldn't blame him. Synda was the only one who was half way on my side. I was shocked that Asha agreed to keep her.

"Everything ok," She said as she looked up at me.

"They let me go."

Bastard police officers. They had locked me in a freezing room for hours—one of their scare tactics. As one's body temperature decreased, symptoms of hypothermia such as shivering and mental confusion usually began to set in. That, along with other unconstitutional tactics, was how the police coerced confessions out of people. And while their limbs were covered by their uniforms, the tank-top, short-shorts and sandals that I had on left my arms, legs and feet exposed to the cool air. It was so cold that each breath of air that I let out momentarily froze before it evaporated. Not to mention the layer of frost that had formed on the stainless steel table at which I was seated. And their no-good asses had the nerve to deny my request for a cigarette. *That's what really pissed me off.*

"Is that you Ms. Felton?" One of the two police officers in the room asked, ignoring my threat and pointing to the activity taking place on the mobile television that they had rolled in on a cart.

"Yeah, that's me. And, so what?"

I stared at me and Pop making our acting debuts in *my porno.* They had confiscated the DVD's at the crime scene. My face was blurred and I could have denied that it was me if they hadn't stripped searched me upon arrival—another example of them violating my constitutional rights since I wasn't officially under arrest. The five-star tattoo on my lower back that they had discovered during the strip search was visible in the DVD. "But, like I said," I continued. "I already told y'all that I was with Pop earlier that day, but they dropped me off at home that evenin'. I don't know anything beyond that point," I lied with a straight face.

Beef and Pop weren't the smartest criminals, but they had learned never to leave their fingerprints behind—the reason we all had put on them hot-ass-wool-winter gloves before entering the mansion. Also, I kept a good weave job; any hairs that the police rounded up as evidence were 100 percent synthetic. Without a confession and an eye witness placing me at the scene of the murders, they didn't have shit on me.

"They let you go…just like that?" she asked.

"Yep."

"That's 'cause you white. Let that have been me."

"What-the-hell-eva. They let me go 'cause I don't know shit and they ain't got shit." Like I said, I had planned on taking the identities of Cream, Pop and the twins' murders with me to the grave.

* * *

194

"Mama?"

Finally, she gotta it right the first time. "Yes, Synda?"

"Can I go outside and play with Sonny and 'em?"

"You can go, but don't be runnin' in and out of Ms. Vett's house."

"Okay."

I followed Synda outside, and walked to Asha's unit.

"Why the hell you got on all them damn clothes?" She asked upon opening the door. "It's a thousand-and-one degrees out there."

Conscious of the real reason for the maturing legions on my legs and slowly coming out of denial, I had thrown on some jeans and a long-sleeved shirt. "I'm just tryin' to cover up my mosquito bites," I said, lying of course.

"Come in, your making me hot."

"I want to thank you and apologize at the same time. I remember we were kinda cool in middle school. Then our lives went in different directions. I really loved Cream, ok. He looked out for me and made me feel like I belonged. I didn't want to let that go, especially after becoming pregnant. When I found out that Cream was in love with someone else, I hated that person. I didn't even know it was you until recently. The truth is I wished so bad to be you in a way," I admitted.

"Why?" she asked.

"Because no matter what you did on the Ave. the people out here still showed you respect. Cream still loved you. I couldn't understand so I hated you and wanted to make you miserable. The whole time I really hated myself." Tears started to pore from my eyes.
She came over to me and rubbed my back. There was truly something different about her spirit. She had an extra pep in her step and excitement in her voice. We talked for a few hours and it turned out we had a lot in common.

"What's got you so happy? I know it ain't no dick 'cause you get that all the time." I joked.

Asha shot up her middle finger before speaking. "I'm goin' to turn my life around and leave the projects for good. I just want more out of life. I want people to look up at me and not down."

"Where the hell you goin'? We just got cool. I didn't know you had cash like that to be movin' somewhere where you actually have to pay rent."

"I don't. A friend is helpin' me out until I find a job."

"A job? Like a real job?"

"Yeah, a real job…a nine-to-five."

"That money comes slow…not your pace."

"And quick money goes fast. I can stand to slow it down a bit."

She's serious, I thought, glancing around Asha's unit. There were several boxes scattered about, old newspapers for the wrapping of breakable items and packing tape. She was leaving all the bullshit behind. Hearing about her new lease on life brought more tears to my eyes. I was genuinely happy for the change she desired to make to better her life. It was too late for me.

There was a knock at the door. Asha went to open it. It was the girl Shonni that Man-Man was with.

"Heyyyy" she said slowly looking at me then back at Asha.

Asha laughed, "We good now. What's up?"

"Where you goin'?" Shonni asked, eyeing all of the boxes.

"I'm movin'."

"You movin'?" Shonni laughed as if the idea of one of us moving onward—was a joke.

"That's what I said. I'm tired of the life I've been livin'. Enough is enough."

"That nigga drivin 'that Porsche got you on some next-level shit, huh? How much you know about him?"

"Really, Asha," I said. "How do you know he's not a serial killer."

"He's black. Ain't he?" Shonni asked, as if she would be stunned to discover he wasn't. *She knows Asha don't discriminate on the avenue.*

"Not that it's any of y'all's business but yes, he's black."

"Well, that let us know he's not a serial killer."

"Niggas kill too," I said.

"We kill people we know...not random mother-fuckers," Shonni argued.

"What about that sniper guy?" I threw back at her.

"We ain't claimin' him."

Asha shook her head, refusing to join in on the conversation. And she didn't have much to share about her friend—just the minute details. His name was Blair. She had met him at K&F. But he wasn't picking her up, just in need of directions. They didn't fuck then and still hadn't which was surprising to me. A nigga not trying to get some ass was always suspect. Or, maybe, he was just a gentleman. And he had money; although, his hustle was still a mystery to Asha. She knew the basics and that's all that mattered. He was paid, wasn't set out to get any pussy and most importantly, he made her want to be a better woman.

"Well," Shonni said, with what sounded like a hint of envy in her voice. "Good Luck."

"Thanks."

"Are you comin' with me to the hospital? I gotta pick up Ki-Ki. She rode in the back of the ambulance with Dream and you know she ain't got no ride back home. Y'all can see the baby too. He's so cute."

"I'll ride," said Asha.

"Can I come," I said.

"Sure." She said.

When arrived at the hospital and stepped off of the elevator and into Maternal-Infant Services, three hospital security guards were holding Ki-Ki back in their arms.

"Tell'er to say somethin' else. My foot gone be in her fat ass."

"Ma'am, please calm down."

The nurse assigned to Dream's care had apparently made an opinionated remark about babies being born too irresponsible, unmarried, young black women while many married and established couples—black and white—struggled to reproduce due to infertility issues.

"Just a shame..." the nurse had said along with stating that she wanted to press charges against Ki-Ki.

"Bitch, press them! Please! I want you to. That's just another reason for me to whoop your ass. My nephew is gone be taken care of...worry about your own damn kids."

The guards explained to the nurse that unless Ki-Ki had physically harmed her, there was no crime committed and therefore no cause to press charges. They also warned Ki-Ki that if she didn't settle down, they *would* have her arrested for disorderly conduct.

The green-eyed monster of a nurse stomped away—glancing at me in the process and probably wondering what a white girl like me was doing in the mix of things. That or she was calling me a wigga in her thoughts. I turned my nose up at her and went to Ki-Ki's aid to let it be known whose side I was on; the side of people I had come to know and love and to the side of people who would accept, love and raise my kids when I was dead and gone.

Asha

Chapter 22

Ki-Ki had wild out all the way out at the hospital. Not even the threat of being thrown in a jail cell had calmed her down—it took an apology from the nurse and a cocktail of sedatives that she gladly swallowed with Dream's hospital apple juice.

"Those damn pills got me feelin' right," she had said as the medication began to take effect.

I laughed at the memory. I was going to miss her the most, but I promised myself that I would visit. I didn't want to be one of those people who made it up and out of the ghetto only to forget where I had come from. *Actin' all brand new and shit. Never that.*

Sitting on top of one of the taped boxes, I looked around my unit. The interior was dated and drab. Shonni's unit was the only one I knew of in East Bridge or any other set of projects in America that had a kitchen with granite countertops, a bamboo floor and stainless steel appliances. *Who, in their right mind, renovates some shit they don't own? Not to mention it's project housin'! Only Shonni.* I figured she had planned on living and dying in projects since she had gotten her sponsors to remodel her unit and fill it with expensive Bassett furniture. I, on the other hand, had finally opened my eyes to the possibility of life outside the four corners of East Bridge and beyond the Avenue—thanks to Blair and Pam. And I had decided that the chances of Blair turning out to be a slimy pimp like Tuffy were slim to none. No pimp was going to invest any time or money into bettering any of his hoes. If anything, a pimp wanted to keep his hoes in the gutter and more than likely strung out; stuck in a place of hopelessness and dependent on him for their every need. *Nah, Blair ain't operatin' no whorehouse. If so, he's the best damn pimp a hoe could have.*

In the middle of packing, I had taken inventory of my own belongings. Outside and inside my unit, I had surrounded myself by things that were deteriorating: a sunken-in dusty orange couch and love seat in the living room along with a coffee table and set of end tables that had peeling brass frames, a round mahogany dinette table in my kitchen that wasn't just chipped but missing chunks of wood out of its' core and wobbly wooden chairs that matched, a six-drawer dresser in my bedroom in which four of the drawers refused to close properly and a broken box spring that barely held up the weight of my mattress. And admittedly, none of the furniture in my unit actually belonged to me. For years I had been there and still was making monthly payments to Rent-A-Center for all of it—paying thousands of dollars in interest for some shit that the Salvation Army wouldn't even take which is exactly what I told the manager of the chain store when I called them to come and pick up *their* shit because I was moving and not interested in carrying any baggage with me.

Besides my clothes, shoes, purses, personal belongings and a few sentimental items, I wasn't taking much with me and didn't necessarily need all of the empty boxes I had gathered. I suppose I wanted to feel like I owned much more than I actually did. *But, hell, there's fifty-year-old niggas walkin' around who didn't own shit...not a home...not a car...not even a pot to piss in.* I was young and still had time. And finally, I was headed in the right direction.

After my impromptu therapy session with Pam, I had left the mission an official enrollee in the program; three months of counseling to cope with my past and classes to prepare me for my future; the process of transitioning from Victim to Dominic. The program also offered additional treatment to those addicted to drugs and alcohol. *Thank goodness I got over my pill habit.* And the reason why I didn't need anything besides the essentials from my unit was because Blair insisted on setting me up in an apartment that he said would be move in ready—fully furnished and supplied with everything from dishes to bed linen. I didn't know the location or if he would be staying there with me on occasion; only that in a few short days' movers were scheduled to pick up the boxes I had packed and to whisk me off to my new life.

The ringing of my cell phone startled me out of my day dream. I was thinking about my future; graduating from the program, getting a job and possibly going to college. However, I was quickly reminded of the bullshit in my present.

Usually I didn't answer UNKNOWN calls but for some reason, I picked up. "Hello."

"Bitch, watch your back because I'm commin' for you."

"Who the fuck is this?" I asked, knowing that the caller on the other end of the line was no one but Tink. I recognized her voice and the buzzing of hair dryers and Jael yapping his mouth in the background gave her ass away. She was calling me from the salon. *What was the point of her callin' me anonymously? Dumb ass.* She had already made up in her mind that I had fucked Dameon. So, there was no use in me wasting my breath trying to convince her otherwise. We were officially beefing.

"Hoe, don't talk about it...be about it." I hung up the phone readier than ever to bounce. And nothing was going to stop me—not even an old friend turned enemy.

* * *

I answered the door ready to rumble with my stun gun tucked in the waistband of my sweats and a bat in my left hand, expecting it to be Tink. Instead, it was Cedric. He had a large white gift box wrapped in red satin ribbon in his hands.

"It's from the boss," he said, handing me the box.

I leaned the bat up against the wall and took the box with both hands, grinning harder than a nigga with a firm grip on Nicki Minaj's ass.

"And be ready at eight. A limo will be waitin' for you."

"A limo?"

Niggas could front if they wanted to, a limo coming into the hood was news worthy. It represented the presence of someone important, rich or famous— tucked away behind dark tint, chilling on plush leather seats and sipping his or her choice of drink out of crystal flutes. *But, shit, anyone who saved their pennies could rent a fuckin' limo.* Still, I was excited.

"Okay, cool," I said to Buff. "I'll be ready."

"Don't be draggin' your feet. The pilot will be ready to take off at exactly eight-thirty."

"Pilot?"

Closing the door behind him, I wasted no time untying the ribbon from around the box. Inside was a short, strapless, A-line, teal blue dress that was identical to the fabric of the ribbon and matching

Christian Louboutin's. *Wait until I show these bad boys to Shonni.* She had several pair, but these were my first. Blair was introducing me to the finer things in life and I hoped that it was all just the beginning.

* * *

The chauffer opened the door for me and I ducked inside the back of the limo. It was as lavish as I had imagined and in that moment, I pretended that I was Cinderella; although, I was fully aware that there were no fairytale endings in the hood. *Only in fantasy land.*

At 8:20 pm exactly the limo pulled into a private hanger at the New East airport where a mid-size Lear jet was gearing up for takeoff. The back door of the limo opened. I stepped out to see Blair standing on the top step of the jet like he was king of the world. He donned a white linen suit and matching white leather Gucci loafers. His arms were stretched wide, welcoming me to come aboard.

"You look stunning." He flashed his million-dollar smile.

"Thanks."

Blair had guessed the right size and picked out the perfect style dress for my figure. Because of my tiny waist, ripe ass and thick thighs, it was always hard for me to find articles of clothing that fit my upper and lower body simultaneously. Shit was either too big in the waist or too tight in the ass.

I placed my hands inside of Blair's. He led me up the stairs and into the Jet. Although there was just the two of us and the pilot, the jet seated seven comfortably. And as the headrests and floor mats of the limo, monogrammed into the headrests of the cream colored seats and coordinating wood grain hardware of the jet were the initials BAR. The same letters tattooed on Blair's upper right arm. The limo nor jet were rented, each belonged to Blair.

I studied his traits of Middle Eastern descent they were all in the structure of his face, skin color and hair. *Only them Sand niggas got more money than Bill Gates and Trump...able to afford jets and shit. He is black*, I concluded about Blair.

We took seats adjacent to each other. "You smell good," he said.

"I taste even better," I responded, trying to get my grown and sexy on and to gauge Blair's reaction. Sometimes he looked at me with desire in his eyes and other times I wondered if he only thought of me as a charity case.

"Who are you?" I asked, leaning into him.

"I like for people to get to know me for the person I am and not for who they think I am or because of what they think I got. In time, you'll know me well enough." Blair winked while popping the cork out of a bottle of champagne and filling our flutes with bubbly. "To us," he toasted.

Did he just say "us"? I had to ask myself before I made a fool of myself. *Maybe he does really like me.* "To us," I repeated and smiled. I had gone from standing on the corner to actually having someone who cared or seemed to care about me in my corner—a man at that.

This made me think about the lies Lynn filled in my head. She would always say men didn't give a fuck about women. I used to tell her my dad loved my mother. She would laugh and say things like, "If you only knew." Whatever that was supposed to mean…

"Fuck these niggas and get what you can get out of them," she would tell me when I was younger and didn't even know what "fucking" was. And the stench that crawled up my nose every time I entered her unit, I learned was sex mixed with liquor and cigarette smoke.

"What the fuck you pinchin' your nose for?" She would always ask me. *Because it stinks in here,* I would always think in my head. And then she would have the nerve to order me to spray some air fresher in every room of the unit.

Just as Blair and I were getting cozy, the pilot emerged from the cockpit and into the cabin. "Sir, there seems to be a problem with the one the fuselage engines. I just don't think it's safe for us to take off right now," he said to Blair.

Oh-hell-nall, I thought. *I am not tryin' to die in a plane crash. Not tonight.*

"I trust you, Captain. No, problem," Blair said, not upset at our change of plans and neither was I. As long as I was with him, I was happy.

The limo driver was back at the hanger in no time. Blair ordered him to take us to the Dupont Hotel where he and Buff were still staying in one the hotel's presidential suites. We had dinner in one of the hotel's five-star restaurants. On our way up to the floor of the suite, I could have sworn that I saw Shonni in one of the hotel's multiple lobbies. *Everybody has a twin*, I thought but quickly reverted back to the naughty thoughts I was having about Blair. For the first time, I would sleep with a man for free.

Shonni

Chapter 23

Even though I was back up a couple of bucks, I still considered myself broke as a motherfucking joke. Yet, nobody could tell me a got damn thing because I stayed fly if nothing else. And I strutted through the lobby of the Dupont Hotel like my shit didn't stink—with the incident of my car almost being repo'd in the distant past. My hips were swinging, my ass was jiggling and my Remi was shining and flowing down my back like The Connect liked. I was wearing a form fitting sleeveless Michael Kors dress. It was short as hell—of course—and my French manicured big toe peeped out of some coordinating black Michael Kors open-toe stilettos. To add some color to my outfit; I topped it off with my cobalt blue Dior clutch. *Trina better step back because I think I'm the baddest bitch*, I thought and swung my hair over my shoulder.

Making my way through the lobby, I thought I had spotted Asha walking hand-in-hand with a nigga—acting like she was all in love and shit. Being farsighted, I couldn't make out the couple's blurred faces as they headed towards the elevators. If it *was* her and the nigga who drove the Porsche, I hoped she hadn't gotten her hopes up too high because project hoes never got wifed. *She should know that...comin' from a line of prostitutes,* I thought, knocking on The Connects suite door.

Just as he did last time, The Connects bodyguard patted me down and searched my purse. There was nothing in it except for my driver's license, keys, lip gloss, a compact mirror and a pack of condoms.

"My lovely, Shonni," He greeted me in the foyer of the suite.

"Guy, it's good to see you again." I hugged him, making sure he felt the warmth of my body. "Manson told me that you put in a special request for my services."

"What can I say? Your pussy, good pussy," he said. "Come. Follow me. I have something special planned for you tonight."

Guy took my hand and guided me down two steps that led into the dimly lit dining area of his suite. *So much for dinner for two.* In the middle of the room was a massive oval-shaped table that seated twelve and every seat was filled except for two empty chairs left unoccupied that I assumed were for me and him. The group around the table could have easily slipped into the White House undetected—posing as a selection of delegates sent to the United States to meet with the

President. They, after all, were associates of Guy which meant they were major players in the universal drug game—moving weight globally. They weren't the type to simply let niggas off with a slap on the wrist if crossed; trust and believe blood was shed.

Oh, shit! It sunk in. I was in the presence of some notorious cartel-kingpin niggas.

"Daddy," I purred in his ear. "I didn't know you had company. I can disappear until you finish your business." I sucked on his earlobe, sneaking a peek behind him and into the vastness of the suite, looking high and low for some Exit signs. There was one way in and one way out of the suite; through the front the double doors. And I wasn't passing through them any time soon.

"Shonni, you are our guest of honor tonight." For a bitch who thought quickly on her feet, I was suddenly speechless and dumbfounded—unable to finagle my way out of the suite.

As we walked toward the empty seats, the "delegation" stood and bowed. *They ain't goin' to the White House dressed like that.* They weren't clothed in suits and ties but completely naked underneath. Instead of walking into a mafia meeting, I now felt like I had interrupted a soiree at a Gentlemen's club; especially since I had eyed the oversized swivel serving tray in the middle of the dining room table with West Indian and other foreign delicacies that no one could pay me a billion damn dollars to eat.

"Have some."

"Ummm…no thanks," I declined his offer. *I thought Manson was over his issue with me. He was going to pay me extra for endurin' this shit.* The men feasted while I looked on in disgust, sipping on the glass of bitter water that had been placed before me.

Spinning alongside of the "food" on the tray was a platter hosting a mound of powdery coke and a bowl full of pills. Guy picked up one of the little purple pills and placed it in the palm of my hand.

I shouldn't have accepted it. Everyone knew my mode of operation; I didn't smoke weed or drink too much in public because I wanted to be conscious and fully aware of my surroundings at all times. I certainly didn't fuck around—sniffing or swallowing shit that I knew nothing about. And if there was ever a time when I needed to be alert, it was the moment I was in—surrounded by men who, at their very core, were ruthless. But, I did it; I popped the pill—figuring it would only be a matter of time before I was forced to do so anyways. And honestly, I needed something to help me shake the image stained in my head of the nigga Heedy had shot and killed slumped over on the floor of Manson's office—gasping for air as he took his last breath. It was much like the coffee stain I had put in my once new couch—permanently. *Post-*

For The Love of It

traumatic stress syndrome is some real shit. If watching one nigga die had such an effect on me, I could only imagine the wages of war on a soldier. *No wonder they come back home all fucked up...mentally disturbed and deranged.*

The pill was no bigger than a tic-tac, yet, it was as powerful as dynamite.

I was feeling lightheaded as if I was losing all control of my senses. I tried to stand, but my balance was off. I began to experience double vision. *One...two...four...* By the time I was done counting, I had counted twenty-two people seated around the table. And my hearing was also distorted. The chatter of the "delegation" sounded like it had been chopped and screwed. It was like some Mike Jones shit. I fell back into the chair that I had been sitting in and grabbed my head. I was losing it; on my way to blacking out. But, for a few more minutes, I was still able to comprehend the conversation and actions taking place around me.

"What else is on the menu for tonight?" asked one of the men.

"My favorite American cuisine," Guy answered, walking towards me. "Soul food," he said, ordering his bodyguard to clear the swivel serving tray and lift my motionless body onto it. Because I was paralyzed by the drug or—in theory—by the decisions that I had made in my life that led me to the moment...there was nothing I could do but lay there. I was helpless.

Guy raised my dress over my hips, exposing my bare body to men looking on. "It turns me on when they don't wear any panties." He pushed my thighs apart and beamed with delight at my Brazilian wax job. "Beautiful." He spread the lips of my vagina apart and sprinkled some coke onto my pussy like he was topping a piece of French toast with some powdered sugar. The two men then began taking turns licking my insides until they had licked all of the coke away.

"Delicious," he said, coming up from between my legs with a ring of my wetness around his mouth.

"Told you," Guy said. The two hi-fived each other.

As Guy and his partner began to undress so did all of the men who were present. They spun my ass around on the swivel serving tray like they were contestants on The Wheel of Fortune, trying to win the big prize. Someone opened my legs to do with my body as he pleased. Each man took his turn to feast upon the main course of the evening...me.

I stared up at the crystals dangling from the extravagant chandelier above the dining room table until everything became all a daze.

* * *

"Senorita. Senorita."

I felt a light tap on my shoulder. "Huh?" I sprung up. "Where am I? What happened?" The woman was an older Hispanic lady. She was wearing a burgundy maid's smock worn by all of the employees of the hotel's housekeeping crew and had a dust mop and roll of trash bags in her hands.

"What's that smell?"

"It's comin' from you, Senorita?" She said, pointing to my bare ass.

I smelled like a week old fish. I was where I remembered last, in the middle of the dining room table on top of the swivel contraption; still in my stilettos but nothing else.

Some may think that I deserved what I got, but that line of thinking was like saying a broad walking down the street naked deserved to be raped. When I fucked a nigga, it had always been on my own terms. The situation would have been different if the conditions were agreed upon; maybe $5,000 per member of the "delegation" for five minutes. *A five-for-five deal.* But, they had violated me—no permission given. And if I died trying...Guy, his partner and every member of the "delegation" were going down. They weren't to be fucked with but neither was I.

Carly

Chapter 24

Getting high should have been the last thing I was doing, but Amber was over and we were smoking the hell out of some weed that she had copped from Heedy. We had smoked the entire contents of one plastic baggie full and were moving on to the next.

My eyes followed Amber's hands as she emptied the filling from a vanilla Game onto my table and proceeded to roll up another blunt, sealing it with her saliva. It was on and popping.

My dreams were still being haunted by Cream, Pop and the twins' murders. And my spirits were down as I faced the likelihood that I probably wouldn't be around for my kid's adult years. On top of all of that, I couldn't shake the feeling that something or somebody was still watching me. *Maybe Manson/Man-Man had sent killers are after me.* But, it could have easily just been my imagination. The doctor at the clinic *did* inform me that experiencing hallucinations was a symptom of having AIDS.

I fired up the first blunt and took a few puffs but before passing it on to Amber, I confessed to her that I had the virus. She shrugged her shoulders as if to say, "So, what." We had smoked so many times together before that if there was a chance of her getting the disease through our extracurricular activity, she would have long been infected. I had no idea who had passed the virus on to me or when. But truth-be-told, it could have been —one of Amber's tired-ass older brothers. I had hooked up with him once, a long time ago; just a few short months after Synda was born. That's around the time Cream started acting up. I was human and lonely. There were a few niggas from South and East Bridge that I had fucked on the low. Her brother had come up a few dollars in a dice game and was looking to spend his winnings on some grown-woman ass, I suppose. I needed the money for some Similac and Gerber's baby food for Synda. So, it went down. If I had gotten the disease from him, then surely Amber had it too—if the rumor of her being molested by her father and brothers were true.

Looking at things vice-versa, as many niggas as I had bedded, I could have infected him and therefore responsible for Amber's bad luck if she *was* infected. It was all too much for my mind to comprehend. I thought I should tell Asha, because she was fucking Cream. Hopefully for her they used condoms. I figured that's why she never popped up pregnant.

I took a long drag from the blunt situated between my thumb and index fingers. Being high was a temporary fix, but it allowed me to escape reality for the time being.

Amber had a confession of her own. *Being high sure will make a broad confess some shit.* She had divulged that she often fantasized about chopping her father and brothers up into tiny little pieces with a butcher knife and feeding their flesh to gutter rats. She said she wanted to stick their dicks in the blender while ass fucking them with a broom. That was some sadistic shit but I could understand why.

"I've been thinkin' about doin' that shit for a very long time. Hell, one day I just might wake up with the guts to do it," She said, blowing smoke out of her nostrils.

"That's some Hannibal Lecter-type shit," I said. "You must really hate them to want them to suffer like that."

"I've suffered at their hands. It would only be what they deserved."

"Well, if you do it, I guess the next time I'll be seein' your ass is in an episode of Snapped."

She and I started laughing and couldn't stop. *Blame it on the weed.* After a few minutes, we were able to calm our giggles down but needed something to satisfy the bout of munchies we felt coming on.

"What you got to eat?" she asked, following me into the kitchen. "Damn, you ain't got shit," she said, looking over my shoulder as I opened the refrigerator and kitchen cabinets. They were back on bare; we were out of groceries once again.

I sighed in relief—glad that Synda was over Ms. Vett's playing. She never sent Synda home with an empty stomach no matter how much she complained about feeding other people's kids. "I got enough damn kids runnin' 'round here to feed," she always said.

We went back into the living room and sat our asses in the same spots they had been in all day, smoking our time away. I had a few yellow xannie bars on deck so we popped them. I flicked on the television and coincidently, the Oxygen channel was running a Snapped marathon.

I surfed through the channels some more, stopping at the sight of a woman with a straw hat on and a sheer blue veil covering her face. Underneath it appeared that her face was mangled.

"What the hell? Her face is fucked up," Amber said, inching closer to the television screen to get a better look.

"Damn," I said, blinking to make sure I wasn't experiencing a hallucination. *Then again, it could have been the weed.* "I wondered what happened to her."

The woman had been attacked by her friend's pet chimp. Her face had been completely mauled. She had also lost her entire right hand up to the elbow and most of the fingers on her left.

"I would have beat that chimp's mother-fuckin' ass."

"And his owner's too," I added.

The show broke for a commercial break. Amber and I just sat back shaking our heads. It was one of the saddest stories I had ever heard. *Beside my own.*

"Can I ask you a personal question?" asked Amber.

"Go 'head."

"How do you feel?"

"About what?"

"About havin' AIDS?"

"Shit, I don't know," I said. "I'm just goin' to wait it out."

"Wait what out?"

"The time I got left until I die."

"If you keep thinkin' like that then you'll be dead tomorrow. You can't give up that easily."

"Just in case you didn't know, there's no cure for AIDS."

"Shit, there ain't no cure for cancer either. But, my mommy fought like hell to live as long as she could. She battled cancer like a giant to stay alive. Not for herself, but for me...her daughter. I think that she knew my father and brothers wouldn't treat me right. They some real scumbags," Amber said, rolling her eyes. She went on, "My mommy held on, but she was tired. I could see it in her eyes. I remember tellin' her that it was okay...that I was goin' to be okay...that she could rest. The next day she passed," Amber said, now with tears in her eyes.

"I'm just sayin', Carly, you have to fight to live...if not for yourself then for your kids, especially Synda"

I took Amber's words to heart. Hearing her describe her mother's will to live touched me along with the strength and courage of the woman behind the veil. She could no longer see, smell, touch or taste. Yet, she wanted to live and remained hopeful about her future. And, I had always heard of people saying that the best thing that ever happened to them was the worst because they learned how to appreciate life even more and their lives usually changed for the better. In my situation, I guess it took catching AIDS to change the way I was living.

* * *

I woke up with a new outlook on my future. Although I was diagnosed with a death sentence, I was going to turn it into a life sentence. *If I only knew how true that statement would turn out to be.*

By 9:30 am there were two messages on my pre-paid Metro phone. One of the messages was from Henrietta Johnson referring me to a counselor at the Porter Health Center encouraging me to come into the clinic to speak with a counselor and of course, they wanted to know if I remembered any of the names of my past sexual partners in order for them to inform the men of my status. It was required by law that they ask. The number of niggas I had fucked was probably equal to the number of hairs on my head, writing their names down in a list would be like writing a novel. It was a task that would take time. *I'm gonna have to get back with them on that.*

The other message was from a broad with the strongest country accent I had ever heard. *She must be from way, way down South...from the backroads.*

"Hi Ms. Felton. My name is Shandra Stevens and I'm your new caseworker." "Yay!" *Did she just say, yay?* I asked myself, listening to the message. "Your old worker was moved to another unit and I was assigned some of her case files." *What...they moved her to a unit for uncompassionate caseworkers who really don't care if their clients starve to death?* I listened to the rest of the message. "I just wanted to call and introduce myself. Please call and set up an appointment so I can see of what assistance I can be to you. Thanks and I look forward to meeting you. Yay!" *She gone have to stop with that yay shit.*

Along with being country, she sounded young and overly excited like a high school cheerleader. However, my instincts told me that she was a new caseworker—eager to get her career with the state started and not yet consumed with an overbearing caseload. *She'll find out soon enough.* Anybody that excited about work was crazy. My old worker would never have acted like she wanted to help me at all. At least, Shandra was making an attempt. It was apparent that she hadn't cracked open my case file and discovered that my benefits had been slashed and that I was under investigation for welfare fraud. *Maybe she can get my benefits reinstated and help me get the meds I need. Maybe even get a job...if anyone will hire me.*

I decided to make a trip down to DHS.

Asha

Chapter 25

Things between Blair and I were moving much slower than they did when I was in the company of a trick. Usually, the whole ordeal was over as soon as I started getting into a good fucking or sucking rhythm, whichever I was paid to do. Truthfully, the majority of tricks I encountered never thanked me for my services at all. They recovered from their nut, pulled up their pants and left; if I hadn't already.

There were some exceptions. Like Doug, husband of the strung-out white woman who used their family minivan to make frequent trips to the hood for her daily fix of pills, who—in turn—had made a trip to the hood himself for some ass obviously because his wife was too occupied with her habit to tend to his needs. He came quick like the others but when it was all over and done, *he* thanked me. *Yeah, Doug was definitely an exception.*

When I thought about sex, I automatically thought about making a profit; Blair had introduced me to the pleasure of it—foreplay, displays of affection and acts of sensuality. The night we shared together was the closet I had ever come to…making love.

* * *

Blair began by gently touching me, brushing my hair to the side and wetting the nape of my neck with short, soft and warm kisses. From my left shoulder to my right, he trailed my back with the same soft kisses while easing the zipper down on my dress. He was situated on the side of the bed, close to the edge, with the first few buttons of his white linen shirt unbuttoned—his growing erection masqueraded under his pants made of the same linen fabric. I stood locked in between his muscular thighs with my back towards him—heels kicked off and to the side.

My dress fell to my feet. If not for the thong I had on, I would have been completely nude. I hadn't worn a half bra with my strapless dress because my young breasts were still perky and now that they had been exposed to the chill in the air, my nipples were as erect as Blair's fully expanded manhood.

He then bent me over, getting rougher by the second as I got wetter. The thong I was wearing had disappeared into the depths of my ass. Blair dug it out, moved it to the side and pushed my butt cheeks apart. And then I felt the warmth of his tongue slithering up and down—from the top of my ass to the bottom. *This nigga is eatin' my ass hole out.* It was something that

Cream used to do—from the back to the front. There wasn't nothing like a nigga with a talented tongue and as I screamed out in pleasure, I knew that I had struck a gold mine. Blair's tongue was worthy of being classified as national treasure.

While dining on my backside, Blair reached around and begins fingering my pussy. If felt like I was having two simultaneous orgasms. I was sure that if I hadn't shown Blair a copy of my test results, indicating that I had tested negative for all STD's, he would not have been as comfortable pleasing me in such a manner because of my not-too-distant past working the boulevard.

I had bumped into Carly at Henrietta Johnsons. I was there for my monthly examine as always. I wasn't for sure why Carly had decided to pop into the clinic, but from the terror in her eyes as she emerged from the back of the clinic, I knew that her test results weren't favorable. I wasn't the only one who had an inkling that the sores consuming her legs weren't mosquito bites; however, no one—especially me wanted to face the truth. Anyone of us could have been infected but being in denial about the possible consequences of our actions allowed us to continue on living irresponsibly. Thank God I used condoms with Cream.

When I showed Blair my test results, I asked him about status. He had no documentation in his wallet to back it up but said that he was clean—recently tested by a doctor working for his insurance company because he had just taken out a hefty life insurance policy on himself and had to go through all of the rigmarole involved, which included being tested for every disease imaginable. I took his word. After all, since he had come into my life, he had only helped not hurt me. I was willing to take the risk.

"Did you enjoy that, baby?" Blair turned me around, lifted me up and laid me down on the bed.

"Yes," I murmured, shifting out of the thong I had on and tossing it on the floor.

Blair was an unselfish lover, taking the time to explore my body. He tasted each of my nipples, slid his tongue down my stomach and then deep into my well. He was thirsty and I had plenty for him to drink.

"You ready, baby?" He asked, retrieving a condom from his wallet that was still inside the back pocket of his linen pants for extra precaution.

"I'm so ready," I moaned, feeling the wetness between my thighs.

Just when I couldn't take him teasing me any longer, Blair gave my body what it was yearning for— his dick. And with each stroke, he discovered spots of pleasure in my body that I didn't even know existed; spots that the tricks I had slept with had left untapped.

* * *

Asha's got a man. I had blown away the layer of dust that had formed on an old Chante` Moore-

Lattimore CD that I had. I was listening to *Chante's Got a Man* off of her third album, *This Moment is Mine.* Of course, I had interjected my name in place of hers as I sang the song. I was singing and skipping around my unit, packing up the last of my possessions and in a state of happiness that I had never experienced before; a state of pure joy that I never believed a broad like me—whose only work experience was being a whore, oh and my short stint at the nursing homes, would ever know in her lifetime. Plain and simple, I was happy as hell.

Blair had dropped me off in front of my unit just a couple of hours earlier. He was off to handle some business matters. I didn't inquire because what he did for a living no longer mattered. Whatever his "business" consisted of, I had decided that I would be down for my man—even if I had to pick up an oozie and shoot a few motherfuckers in his defense.

Before exiting the car, we lean in and kissed each other goodbye. I wasn't oblivious to the fact that a nigga like Blair, apparently paid and fine as hell, could possibly and probably did have other broads on deck. But, this moment was mine.

"The movers will be by tomorrow," he had informed me before speeding away.

"Okay, cool. I'll be ready."

My plan for the day was to spend some time with my new "friends" today since I wasn't for sure the next time I would have a chance to see them again after I moved and got too heavily involved in the program.

While prancing around my unit, throwing a pair of shoes in a box that I had simply labeled SHOES and tossing some belts and hats in another box that I had labeled MISCELLANEOUS, I glanced at the television. The news channels had long stopped covering the Greenville murders and had moved on the latest slaying in the city.

The police were leading a nerdy looking white man from a small brick house in handcuffs. *They always arrestin' some-damn-body.* I un-muted the volume and learned that the suspect had shot and killed his mother while she was sleeping. *Well, damn, I guess his ass needed to be arrested.* The camera zoomed in on the suspect's face. *Hell, nall. I knew his pocket-protector-wearin'-ass was crazy.* It was Pete, the young trick who couldn't pay me to fuck him. When I told him that I was done prostituting myself out, I meant it. *His chances of ever gettin' some pussy are fo'sho over now. He's goin' straight to prison.*

Carly banged on the door.

"Damn. A light knock would have sufficed. I ain't deaf."

"My bad."

"Hey, Asha."

"Hey, little one. Hey Carly, what up?"

"Could you do me a favor and watch her while I run to DHS, I think I can get my stamps back." She pleaded.

I looked down to the doe-eyed child. How could I say no to such a cutie.

"Sure-that's not a problem."

I opened the door and let her in. Carly hugged and kissed Synda goodbye and headed for the bus stop in a hurry. I knew the feeling. If you didn't make it down to DHS early, you had to be prepared to stay all damn day long.

"You hungry?" I asked Synda closing the door behind Carly.

"Yep."

I should have known, last time I watched her that fridge and cabinets were bare as shit. "I'll fix you a bowl of Cheerios and then later we'll go have lunch."

"Okay," Synda said, following behind me. After getting her settled at the kitchen table, I left her to go get showered and dressed. But, half way down the hall, there was another knock on my door.

"You want me to go get your bag?" Synda asked with a mouth full of Cheerios, inching up behind me at the door. She had remembered the last time she was over and I had asked her to go get my purse at the sound of someone knocking at the door. *Kids remember every damn thing,* I thought and laughed.

"No, thanks, princess," I said, looking through the peephole and seeing that it was the Detective.

"I won't be needin' my stun gun. Go finish eatin' your cereal."I opened the door.

"Asha, how are you?"

"I'm good, Detective."

"You want to come out to the cruiser and talk?" He asked, also remembering the last time I encountered him. "I have news about your parent's case."

"No, you can come in. Excuse the mess. I'm movin'."

"Where to?"

"Actually, I don't know. But, anywhere is better than here."

He nodded his head in agreement and took a seat on the loveseat. I faced him, taking a seat on the couch.

"What you got for me, Detective?"

"Good news."

"Really?"

"Your parent's killer is behind bars."

"You arrested him? Where? When? Who is he?" I ranted off.

"No."

"No…you haven't arrested him yet? What the hell are you waitin' on? Y'all out there arresting every-damn-body else."

"Asha, calm down. He's already behind bars."

"Huh?" I asked with a confused look on my face.

"He's been in prison for the last year. His name is Billy Crews."

He went on, "He was convicted and sentenced to two years in prison on an assault and battery charge and human trafficking about a year ago. Thankfully, for us, he's a big talker…wants everyone to think he's this macho-tough guy. Anyways, he confessed to his cellmate that he had raped and murdered a black prostitute and her pimp husband some years back. He described the whole scene detail by detail. He also admitted to killing another prostitute years later and leaving her body in Braggs park. It was all a part of his initiation into a white supremacy organization known as the New Breed."

Flashing back to the moment Lynn reached for Bill's door handle, I suddenly remembered—clear as day—seeing a tattoo of a Nazi swastika on his arm. *How did I forget that?* She had seen the same and must have sensed his evil intentions.

"The state prosecutor, is going to move forward with charging him with your parents and aunts murder. We're goin' for the electric chair."

"I can't believe this. My parents and aunt was killed by the same man…." I was confused and needed answers. The part about my mother being a prostitute and daddy being her pimp messed me up. We didn't live that way. My parents were happy - wait a minute.

233

Daddy did take mom and her girlfriends out a lot and they did wear fancy revealing dresses. I never recalled either one of them having a "real" job. Oh my God it can't be.

"Yes, are you ok Ms. Thomas?"

Hearing this news was more emotional for me than I had anticipated it would be. My eyes began to water as I thought about the most important lesson that I had learned from Blair thus far—that a person's past could be forgiven.

𝔖𝔥𝔬𝔫𝔫𝔦

𝕮𝔥𝔞𝔭𝔱𝔢𝔯 26

An entourage of emergency response vehicles was blocking the main entrance into East Bridge; an ambulance, Ki-Ki truck and multiple police cruisers. *What the hell?* I asked myself, seeing all of the flashing lights. I had to park the Lexus around the block and walk through some neighboring houses in order to get to my unit. Smelling like kitty litter, I hadn't planned on taking any detours; just going straight home and hopping in the shower.

"Shonni!"

Damn it.

"Shonni! I know you hear me." Ki-Ki was calling me over to her unit. Her and Dosha were outside being nosy and looking on at all of the commotion. Dosha had a cigarette hanging from her lips and a red plastic cup filled to the rim with an alcoholic mixture of some sort—I could smell the strong odor of liquor. I stole a glance at the time on my cell phone. It was mid-morning. *Her ass drinkin' already.* But, hell, I was

235

badly in need of a drink myself—considering the trauma I had endured.

"What the hell is that smell?" Dosha asked. "You smell that?"

"Damn, Shonni! You smell like you belong in a tank at Sea World," Ki-Ki said and laughed.

"I got some Summers' Eve if you need it," Dosha offered.

"Fuck both y'all. What happened?" I asked, changing the subject and pointing at all of the chaos.

"Spirit stabbed Tim," Ki-Ki said, swatting at a mosquito that was circling over her head.

"Umm-hmm…caught him messin' around with her cousin Teena like she had suspected." Dosha took a sip from her drink.

"He dead?" I asked, looking at Spirit being led away in handcuffs to a police cruiser. She was cussing and fussing the entire way.

"Fuck no, she just pricked his ass. He don't even need stitches…got the po-po's over here for no reason. I can't even cop no percs." Ki-Ki just shook her head at the nonsense.

"I thought somethin' serious went down," I said, making my way down the sidewalk and across the street to my unit, waving goodbye.

"Make sure you wash that stank cooch," Ki-Ki yelled out.

I paid her no mind, anxious to do just that and get to Manson's trap house; he was expecting me.

* * *

"Ska-daddle." Man-Man waved Jella off like she was a stray dog as he buckled his belt.

"Bitch Bye!" I said, entering his office.

"You got your nerves to be callin' somebody a bitch," Jella said, getting up from off of her knees and wiping her mouth. Manson had her young ass tamed already. *I bet she can't suck him off like me...*

"I guess it takes one to know one." I rolled my eyes at her.

"Man-Man," she started whining. "I'm getting tired of these hoes coming in here disrespecting me."

"Bitch, get the fuck outta here!" Manson and I said in unison.

"Shonni and I have business to discuss."

"You heard that, didn't you?"

"That's okay. You gone get yours just like your girl Asha gone get hers."

There she goes startin' some shit. "Bitch, if I'm gone get mines then why don't you give it to me right now. Yo ain't sayin shit bitch, jump!" I said, stepping to her.

Jella scooped up her belongings and left, sensing that I was done talking and ready to trash her ass.

"Before it's over with, I'm gone end up fuckin' her up...."

"Do you- She still gone suck my dick re-gardless…even if she in a full body cast," Manson laughed.

I took a seat, looking around. His office floor had been buffed, waxed and shined. If I hadn't witnessed a murder take place inches away from where I was sitting, I would have never suspected that the floor—not too long ago—had been coated in blood and tissue matter. It made me wonder how many niggas' souls were floating around in the air above us.

Man-Man slid a stack of one hundred dollar bills across his desk towards me—the remainder of my payment for hooking up with The Connect. I didn't know how much it was but no matter the amount, it wasn't enough for my troubles.

"Did you know there was goin' to be thirteen more motherfuckers in Guys company at the hotel…all waitin' to gang rape me?"

"What the fuck you talkin' 'bout, Shonni?"

I rehashed all that I could remember of the last 24 hours, holding back my emotions at times. No designer bag, shoes or outfit; no major appliances or furniture; no luxury car or even all the money in the world could soothe how violated I felt. Guy and his friends had become my enemies and I wanted them taken care of.

"Shon," Manson replied. "You was fucking me, Nic, Neil and who knows who else was running up in that pussy. You a hoe. How can you let the words gang rape slip from those lips," he laughed.

"Real talk-*Man-Man*," I sighed and giggled. "But how does a gorilla escape from the damn zoo?" I asked, referring to his ape looking ass. There was a time I thought this nigga looked like Tyrese, but that had to be the money. "I don't care how many niggas went up in my pussy, no one deserves to be raped...period. Them Haitian niggas raped me and I want them all dead."

"Run that by me again."

"Nigga! Did you not hear what the fuck I just said? I want Guy hurt-merked-put in the mother fuckin dirt-dead."

Manson reclined back in his black leather office chair, resting his feet on top of his desk and clasping his hands behind his head. He was in thinking mode. Unlike what was on my mind—avenging being drugged and raped fourteen times—he was mentally calculating whether or not Guy was more valuable to him alive or dead. I was hoping for the latter. Long term, it probably wasn't the best decision for Manson—literally severing his relationship with his international connect. Short term, he could hit Guy up for his current inventory and make himself a cushy profit that would last him a while...

Manson was still silent; still thinking. *This nigga right here*, I thought, waiting impatiently for his answer and sure that my proposition wasn't the first time he had tossed the idea of getting rid of Guy and robbing him of his stash of Power. The drug was taking over the streets.

Man-Man took his time weighing out his options. To occupy mine, I stared at him. *I swear money works wonders for a nigga.* I had always believed that. Manson had come a long way too. He was not cute by anyone's standards but since like I said money makes me cum and sometimes dumb. If he was broke I would have never fucked this nigga, even though his dick game was serious. But fuck that, he tried to kick me when I was down, this is strictly business.

"What's up, Shonni?" Heedy walked into Man-Man's office, emptying his pockets and dumping wads of cash in the middle of money on his desk.

"Too much," I said.

"Heedy, ain't it funny that just a few months ago I was strung out over this half-breed boogie bitch. I was about to pop that question and everything. I thought I found a rose in the concrete. I looked out for her bastard ass kids, because I was in my bag. Turns out she was fucking my lawyer, the mayor and me, she ain't no different than the hoe Asha across the street," Man-Man laughed.

I laughed with him, I refused to let him get to me. That nigga was in his feelings. I wouldn't have ever married his ass anyway; his bank account wasn't deep enough.

Heedy didn't know how to respond; so I changed the subject.

"You know Guy and his friends raped me?"

Heedy's mouth dropped. "Damn, Shonni. I'm sorry. That's some fucked up shit to do. You alright?" He asked, genuinely concerned and more fazed by the news than Man-Man.

"What you think? Should we shut Guy's operations down for good?"

"You askin' me?" Heedy pointed at his sixteen-year-old chest.

"Yeah, you. You a lieutenant in this camp. What you think matters," Man-Man gassed him up.

Heedy searched his face for the answer he thought Man-Man wanted to hear. "Shit, I'm down for a witch doctor slayin'. Let's get it.," Heedy said and then looked at me. "And what he did to you was some foul ass shit to do. Any nigga that hurts you needs to pay." He added.

"With his life," I added.

"It's settled then. I'll set up a transaction with Guy…tell'em that I want to buy him and all of his boys out…everythin' they got in stock. We're goin' in for the kill," Man-Man flashed his grill. "But, Shonni," his tone turned serious. "When a nigga goes in for the kill…he or SHE," he stressed, "has to be prepared to kill…or…to be killed. That's just how the game works, Ma."

* * *

Leaving Man-Man's trap house, was the same middle-aged black woman I had seen days before. Again, she was handing out pamphlets to anyone who would take one and for those who stopped to listen, she had a mouthful. I tried to sneak by her but she caught a glimpse of me.

She offered me a pamphlet. "You should think about enrollin' in the Take Your Life Back Program. We can help you change your life around…get you on the right path."

"No thanks," I declined the pamphlet and her help.

"Here." She crammed the pamphlet in my hand. "Just take it. You might change your mind."

She moved on to badger some of the trap boys on the corner and I headed towards my car. Instead of waiting to get home to fix me a drink, I cracked the seal on the Patron and downed half of the bottle in one gulp—sitting behind the steering wheel of my car and thinking that instead of getting the best of my hustle, I had let it get the best of me. The plan to take down Guy, his cousin and the delegation had been set in motion. There was no turning back. Bullets were scheduled to fly and it was going to be their lives or ours. I took another swig of the Patron and started the ignition.

Carly

Chapter 28

Stepping off the Dart bus, the first thing that caught my eyes was a flyer stapled to a utility pole next to the bus stop. *If you have any information regarding the murders of The Hawkins Twins please contact Crime Stoppers at 302-CRIME. The Hawkins family is offering a $15,000 reward for the tip that leads to the arrest of the person(s) involved.*

A picture of the twins in their high school football uniforms was printed on it. They were smiling— standing side by side like giants and both palming footballs; the golden eggs that were going to propel them into collegiate and professional athletic stardom. There was no mention of the other life lost—Pop's. I assumed that Pop's mother probably didn't have the funds to contribute to the campaign.

Facing my own mortality, I was reminded of the value of life. And as shiesty as Beef and Pop were, no one's life deserved to be cut short; including Creams *302-CRIME.* I repeated in my head.

I trekked on to DHS under the hot morning sun, praying that the wait wasn't going to be long before I got in to see Shandra, my new caseworker. Even though I had made an appointment, the flow always seemed to get backed up at DHS. It never failed.

Synda was spending the day with Asha and she was happy to be doing so. She had laid out her clothes and everything. *My little lady.* I didn't know how she was going to take the news of Asha moving. I hadn't broken it to her yet, but her little mind was guaranteed to start spinning when she spotted the taped-up boxes in Asha's living room and a thousand questions were sure to follow. I wondered how close Synda really was with Asha. Maybe Cream had been taking her over there without me knowing. I wasn't sure, all I knew is that my child had a connection with her.

Thinking more about Asha moving—hell—we were just about to kill each other a month ago and now I didn't want her to leave. Life was funny as shit. I guess you never know how a person truly affects you.

The line to enter DHS extended outside the building's glass doors. They had one security guard padding people down, searching their belongings and checking their ID's; doing it all by himself. *The state is so damn cheap. They need to hire some more motherfuckers up in here.* I huffed and puffed. It took me close to twenty minutes to get inside.

I signed in at the clerk's desk and announced my presence. "Carly Felton to see Shandra Stevens."

"Okay, we'll let her know you're here."

"Thanks."

I took a seat in one of the blue chairs. *I should have brought a pillow or somethin'*, I thought—knowing my ass was going to be hurting once I got up as it always did.

"Carly Felton!"

Already? I hadn't been sitting down ten minutes before a young, petite, brown-skin broad with short hair appeared from behind the "Employee-Only" door that led to the case workers' cubicles. It went to show that the congestion at DHS and other state run agencies was partly due to employees procrastinating and in no hurry to do the jobs they were getting paid to do.

"Hi! Ms. Felton. I'm your new caseworker," She said with a welcome smile and full of enthusiasm. *Here she goes.* I thought for sure she was going to break out into a cheer and end her introduction with a "Yay!" But, she kept her excitement tamed.

"Hi!" I said and smiled with just as much energy as she had emitted. Her positive attitude had apparently rubbed off on me. *It's amazin' how that works.*

"Follow me."

Her cubicle smelled of Vanilla Lavender carpet freshener. She had a rug on the floor along with a plant and a dimly lit lamp on her desk; her cubicle was inviting.

Aligned on a shelf above her desk were pictures of her with friends and family. I didn't know much about black sororities or white ones for that matter, but I was sure she belonged to one because in many of her pictures she was throwing up a pinky finger.

She spoke and I directed my attention to her. "Ms. Felton, as of right now, you're case is still under fraud investigation. Those things can take time. But…"

I cut her off. "Here's the deal. I have an eight-year-old daughter and two others, I have no means of feedin' them. I'm not workin' and while I acknowledge in the past that I was able-bodied and should have been workin' instead of abusin' the system…the past is the past and there's nothin' I can do about it. For extra money, I did let other people use my mother's EBT card in exchange for cash…call it fraud if you want to…I was just tryin' to survive. And, well…occasionally, I may have slept with a couple of guys for some cash…well…more than a couple and more like frequently. But, I've just been diagnosed with AIDS and I can't continue on with the fucked up life I've been livin'." Tears began to form in her eyes. *Yep, she's new.* "Girl," I paused my rant and tried to console her by touching her shoulder. "My story may be the first tragic-ghetto-hood one you've heard so far, but I guarantee you that it won't be the last if you keep workin' here. I just hope that you turn out to be a better caseworker than some of your peers and find a way to help others before they get to where I'm at. All I'm askin' for is some help. I need food, my meds and somebody to help me live the rest of my life...however long I have left...on the right track."

She grabbed a tissue from the Kleenex box on her desk and dabbed her eyes.

"You cool?" I asked her.

"Yeah, I'm okay and I'm goin' to help you in every way that I can."

Yes!

* * *

Under state policy, any DHS client under fraud investigation was prohibited from receiving any government assistance. But, she went over and beyond—making phone call after phone call—trying to find me the help I needed. And, she did. An organization called Connections agreed to supply my meds for six months; she gave me the address to the Salvation Army for food and I had an appointment with a woman named Pam to possibly get enrolled in a program called Take Your Life Back for counseling and job Social Security to see if I was eligible for disability being that employers were subject to deny me employment because of my health status.

After leaving DHS, I headed directly to Connections and completed some paperwork and then to the Salvation Army where the Take Your Life Back office was located. Searching the building for the woman that she had referred me to, I came across the finest nigga I had ever seen in Wilmington. He was so fine that he had me stuttering. *If Asha and Shonni could see what I'm seein' right now.*

"I...I...I'm...lookin' for...umm...Pam," I said, peeking my head inside the office next door to the one designated as the INTAKE OFFICE. It was hard for me to take my eyes off of the man behind the desk, but I glanced at the framed magazine covers hanging on the walls of his office. He had been on the cover of Black Enterprise, Forbes and the one I was most familiar with, BALLIN'. He also graced the covers of ESPN and Sports Illustrated. The headlines on all of the magazines read virtually the same, *Billionaire Baller*: *How Blair Roberts is Turning Millions into Billions and Giving Back.* There was also a framed jersey—Roberts 28—also hanging on the wall.

He stood up from behind the desk. "Pam's out to lunch. Is there anything that I can help you with?"

I can think of several things. "Umm...my... ugh..."

I had to get my mind right before uttering another word. By the way that I was drooling, one would have thought that the actor from *Daddy's Little Girls* was standing in front of me. *With his fine self.* The movie was one of mine and Synda's favorites. I had copped a bootleg copy of it but loved it so much that I ended up buying the DVD from Best Buy.

I cleared my throat. "My caseworker sent me over here to talk to her about enrollin' in the Take Your Life Back program."

"Oh, okay. Well, Pam does handle our enrollment processes, but I know a thing or two," he said, reaching for a packet of stapled paperwork. "You can follow me."

Enjoying the view from behind, I followed him down the hall and into a small conference room.

"She should be back momentarily," he said, pulling out a chair for me. *Just when all women thought chivalry was dead.* "I'll send her in…just complete as much of the paperwork as you can. Oh, and, did you need any water or anything?"

"No, I'm good."

"Good. Oh, I don't think I got your name."

"Carly." I extended my hand.

"Nice to meet you, Carly. I'm Blair, CEO and founder of the Get Your Life Back program." he said, shaking my hand.

Blair? Asha's Blair?

"We have offices scattered throughout the East Coast. I'm hoping to expand in the west soon." Instead of leaving me alone to fill out the paperwork he had handed me as I thought he was about to do, Blair took a seat at the conference table. "You know, Carly, there isn't any circumstance that you can't rise above from. I was raised by my grandmother. Both my mother and father were in and out of jail and on and off drugs...junkies. They were never clean long enough to straighten themselves out. My grandmother made sure that I stayed in school and got involved in sports and afterschool activities. When basketball and football seasons were up, she had me takin' ballet lessons and playin' the flute...anything to keep me off the streets," he laughed.

"Sounds like she loved you a lot," I said.

"Yeah, she did. And, I loved her. She was my heart." He pounded his chest. "Anyways, as I got older, I managed to stay out of trouble. Although, I wanted to knock some niggas heads off for teasin' me about my kicks. Everybody was wearin' Jordans while I was rockin' the latest Payless special...the new Pro-wings'. I can laugh about it now," he said. "I was cool up until my senior year in high school. I needed some new football cleats and my grandmother just couldn't afford them. I was too ashamed to ask my coach or anybody else. So, one day I cooked up what I thought was the recipe for some crack. I mixed up all kinds of ingredients. I'm talkin' 'bout flour, sugar, bakin' soda, laundry detergent, bleach...anything and everything white," he laughed again. "I went out and stood on the corner. My first customer rolled up. I handed him a small bag with the white substance in it and he pulled out his police badge. He was an undercover cop."

I sat with my mouth gaped open. "Whaaaattt!"

"Because I didn't have any priors and because the drugs I attempted to sell weren't the real thing, the judge let me off easy. However, after my senior year…a record-breakin' year on the football field, the only university that offered me a football scholarship was the University of Delaware. All the others passed me up because of what happened. They didn't want any so-called troublemakers on their squads. Well, I went on to get drafted into the NFL…been playing for a few years now and just got traded to the Ravens. I love football, but my passion is helping people. With money from some investments of mine I started the Take Your Life Back program a few years back. We're helping more people every year." I thought about the twins and how far they would have gone in their careers and all of the people they might have gone on to help. "I'm glad to be back in the community that accepted me from the beginning…having business meetings with the governor, mayor and community activists…just trying to do what I can to give back."

"I'm sure the city's glad to have you back."

"Seems like it and I've meet a nice young lady that I'm interested in." Blair was talking to me as if we were old friends. "She's special...truly one of a kind. Her name is Asha."

"That's an interestin' name," I said, not acknowledging my association.

"Yeah, I like it. It's different and so is she."

"She's a lucky girl...especially to have caught your eye when a man of your caliber has probably crossed paths with many smart and beautiful women."

"Yeah, well, just because a woman is beautiful on the outside doesn't mean that she's beautiful on the inside. I've met and been with my fair share of women...beautiful and accomplished. But in the end, their true colors always shined. They just wanted the fame and the money that comes with my lifestyle...never really me. And to be honest, they never seemed to need me unless I was buying them gifts or taking them on expensive trips and stuff. Sometimes a man needs to feel emotionally needed. They were always off on that I-don't-need-you tip. Most of the women I've dated just moved on to the next player."

"Some real groupies, huh?"

"You could say so."

"Asha has a past, but who doesn't? She was actually working down on New East Avenue when we met," he said.

"A prostitute?"

"Yeah, well, there's no shame in my game. T-Pain is in love with a stripper and me...I'm falling for a prostitute...ex-prostitute." He joked. "At first, I just wanted to talk to her...tell her about the program and give her a pamphlet when I spotted her. But, I figured she would just shoo me away. I needed an excuse, so I stopped and asked for directions. As soon as I looked into her eyes, I just knew that she was different...that she really didn't want to be on that corner selling her body. She just needed help escaping the cycle she was trapped in. We're still getting to know each other, but I don't see my future without her."

I smiled—truly happy for my new friend. "I'm sure she doesn't see hers without you either."

* * *

Salvation Army was my last appointment for the day. They gave me a box full of canned goods, cereal and other non-perishable items along with a gift card to Wal-Mart for eggs, Cream, cheese, meat and other perishable items that they didn't keep stocked in their warehouse.

I sat the box and grocery bags on the kitchen counter and pulled out some pots and pans—not one of them matched the other. *I'm a have to go to Target and get me a nice set.*

I was preparing to cook dinner for my child— something that I hadn't done in a long time; pork chops along with the instant mashed potatoes, peas and

253

corn that I had received from the food closet. I rinsed off the meat and realized that I didn't even have the bare essentials needed to cook a properly seasoned meal; salt and pepper. It was shameful.

"Synda! Princess!" I yelled from the kitchen, hoping she heard me. *She's probably in there splashin' all kinds of water and soap suds on the floor.* I had picked her up from Asha's on my way into my unit. Of course, she didn't want to leave. I had to practically drag her home. "I'm goin' next door real quick to Dreams to borrow some salt and pepper. Be back in two minutes!"

"Okay!" She yelled back.

No sandwich or cereal tonight, babygirl, I thought heading next door to Asha's. I promised myself that I would start cooking more but most importantly that I would be a better mother; a good mother.

It had been a good day and I was expecting it to be an even better night.

Asha

Chapter 29

After chauffeuring Carly and Synda out the door, I stretched out on the couch with every intention of checking out the issue of Bout that Life' that I had been meaning to read since swiping it from Shonni a while back. Basketball-player-turned-rapper Ron Artest was on the cover and featured in an article entitled, *Ballin' Out of Control.* I couldn't help but remember his post-game interview after the last NBA championship. I didn't watch the game—being that I wasn't a sports fanatic—but caught a short snippet of the interview on YouTube. *That nigga thanked his hood, psychiatrist and promoted his CD,* I thought and laughed out loud. *He crazy....*

After flipping through a few pages of advertisements and before I could read the first article, I had dozed off—waking up minutes later to what sounded like rocks colliding with my living room window. *Ain't nobody but Spirit's bad ass kids ...need to be at home in the bed.* They had been running wild ever since the police had picked her up on domestic abuse charges and there was no telling where Tim's skinny ass was.

"Break my window if y'all want to," I screamed, stumbling off of the couch. I opened up the door without peeping through the blinds or the peephole first and without retrieving my stun gun—two things I rarely did. "I'm a break my foot off in y'all little asses! And I'm tellin' y'all's mama." *As soon as she gets out of jail.*

I took a step outside the door and looked around. There was no one there; at least not in plain sight. Turning back to head into my unit is when I heard them - gunshots. Adrenaline pumping, I rushed down the hallway of my unit—attempting to take cover. *These niggas shootin'. I can't wait until tomorrow when the movers show up. I'm gone be out this hell hole.* Halfway down the hall, I collapsed onto the floor, looking down at a growing red stain on my shirt. It was blood—spilling from my body and dripping into the fibers of the carpet underneath me. I had been shot.

Face up and laying down on my back with my hand clutching the bullet hole in my abdomen, I thought about the years I had spent degrading myself on the Ave, the energy that I had wasted hating Lynn and the joy that I had experienced during the last few weeks of my life—meeting and getting to know Blair and the positive changes that he was inspiring me to make. *Change—for the unlucky—always came a little too late.* And then I thought about Synda and the great day we had spent together.

She had worn me out. We had hit up the movies, the mall and the park where she had me spin her around on the Merry-Go-Round a thousand times, push her on the swings for an hour, and play kickball with a deflated soccer ball that had been abandoned at the park—all until every inch of my body ached.

"Asha, why are all those boxes in your livin' room? Are you movin'?" Synda had asked while we were taking a much needed break on a park bench and sipping the juice out of the "red" snow cones I had purchased us from the ice cream truck that circulated the park.

"Well, the answer to your question is yes. I want to move and try to make a better life for herself," I said.

"Shouldn't everybody in the projects want to move then? Shouldn't you want me to go with you so that I can have a better life too? My daddy always said one day we were all gonna get out of here. You, me, Symia and him…," Synda said, looking up at me with her mesmerizing hazel eyes and licking her snow cone. She had stomped and tore me to pieces with her line of questioning. "Sometimes I wish that you were my mama and not Carly," she added, taking me back to when I was her age and constantly prayed for a new mommy myself. *Anyone*, I thought, would be better fit than Lynn.

"Synda," I turned to face her on the park bench. "Carly is your mother…she loves you very much and she promised me that she's going to try and be the best mother ever."

"Did she really?" Synda perked up.

"Yep, she sure did."

"Do you believe her?" Synda sulked back down onto the bench.

Honesty, I wasn't for sure if Carly was serious about changing her ways and devoting herself to upping her parenting skills or if it was just another promise that would soon be broken. But, I was hopeful. "Yes…I do," I answered Synda. "And…I promise to visit you regularly and come to as many of your school events that I can. I'll always be a part of your life."

"Pinky swear?" Synda held out her hand.

"Pinky swear," I said as we locked pinkies.

Laying shot on the floor all I could think about was that if I died I would be breaking my promise to Synda.

I turned my head to the side—still covering my wound with my hand—and saw the shadow of someone lit against the hallway wall slowly approaching. With what little strength I could muster, I lifted my head, staring into the face of my shooter.

"Ummph," I smirked and rested my head back down on the carpet—staring up at the popcorn ceiling of my unit. *Un-fuckin'-believable!* Over the years, I had had my run-ins with the significant others of tricks I had serviced—never anything that I couldn't talk, scratch or claw my way out of.

One night while I was working the corner I was approached by a broad with a newborn in a filthy onesie—stained with baby food and vomit—on her hip and two barefoot toddlers by the hand. *Who the fuck is this?* I asked myself as I saw her—stomping and cussing down the boulevard like she was about to beat somebody's ass.

"You sleepin' with my man?"

"Which one of us are you talkin' to?" I asked, standing next to Janelli.

"You," she said, adjusting the newborn on her side.

Apparently, she had overheard her man on the phone with one of his niggas bragging about how he smashed a fine-ass-dark-skin hoe with some good-ass pussy on Cash Ave.

"I probably hooked up with him a time or two, but I usually don't catch the names of the tricks I fuck," I had said in a calm demeanor.

She stood in front of me, seemingly busted and disgusted by my candidness. "Well, his name is Doc... if you happen to catch it the next time he comes down here tryin' to buy some loose, prostitute pussy tell him that his daughter needs some pampers and P.J. and Tre need new shoes while he down here trickin' off his entire got damn check." *If that nigga just bringin' home $250 a week then you need to find you another baby daddy,* I thought and wanted to say.

"Will do," I said and turned to finish the conversation I was having with Janelli.

"Hoe," the broad said, turning to stomp her ass back down the block with her kids in tow. *She know she wrong for bringin' them damn kids out here this time of the hour...tryin' to confront somebody about her no-good-ass-broke baby daddy.* I laughed the incident off.

And then there was my run-in with Redd—a Latino tranny from North Philly with reddish, burgundy dyed hair that hung to the crack of his ass—his trademark; hence his name. He had tried to fight me over his cheating ass boyfriend, but I wasn't having it.

When Redd walked, he always swayed his hips like he was about to break out in the Salsa—switching hard enough to knock one of his hips out of socket—just like old ass Jael. And both of them were forever trying to squeeze their Big Foot-size-ass-boat feet into some stilettos. They were also known for trying to fool niggas around the city into thinking that they were all woman—tucking and taping their dicks between their legs with duct tape. I shook my head. Jael couldn't fool any-damn-body with his masculine build and facial structure. But Redd was tall, thin and swan-like with feminine features, except for his massive feet. He attracted many niggas as most Latino transsexuals did.

Redd had actually been keeping surveillance on his nigga. He saw him pick me up from the Avenue and then followed us to the Days Inn. I guessed that the nigga had gotten tired of sucking on Redd's fake-ass silicone implants and grew weary of pretending that he didn't notice the extra set of balls in bed. He came to the Ave looking for a natural born woman, finding me.

Redd gave me just enough time to collect my payment before busting through the hotel door with a plastic fork in his hands; it was the only sharp object that he could find in his car. *What the hell he gone do with that? He would have been better off goin' with an ink pen.* He lunged towards his nigga with the fork in his hand. *Oh...okay...he's goin' for the jugular.* As the two wrestled, one of his press-on nails popped off and into the air. He then dropped the fork and accidentally stepped on it, snapping it in two. Despite his feminine appearance, Redd was all man.

His nigga fell backwards and hit the side of his head on the edge of the hotel bed's wooden headboard. He was down for the count. Redd caught his breath and then turned to me.

I yanked up a lamp from the closest nightstand since my taser wasn't in reach. "I'll knock your ass unconscious, cut your throat open and shave down your humongous ass Adam's apple if you lay one hand on me."

"Fuck you," he said. "You ain't worth me breakin' another nail over anyways." I eased out of the hotel room, leaving him to torture his nigga some more.

I had escaped both incidents and others with a scratch. *Guess this is the last run-in of my life,* I thought, growing weak as more and more blood drained from my body from the gunshot wound. My injury may not have been life threatening but without immediate medical attention, I knew that it was only a matter of time before I bled to death.

Panicked, my shooter dropped the gun at her side—luckily, it didn't go off. She knelt down beside me, smelling of burnt crack cocaine. She was bone thin and her ratty blonde hair looked like it hadn't been washed in months nor did the too-big shirt and shorts she was wearing. I looked at the strung out white woman, soccer mom turned pill head, suburban housewife gone hood, driver of the white minivan and wife of Doug—the only trick that ever thanked me for my services and the city's D.A. who the Detective informed me would be prosecuting my parents and Lynn's killer. Somehow—in between getting high, attending PTA meetings and soccer games—she had found out that I had fucked her husband.

"Oh my God! Oh my God!" She screamed. "What have I done?" *You shot me is what the fuck you did!* I thought and wanted to scream but couldn't find the strength.

"What's your name?" I asked in a low whisper.

"Paula...." she answered.

"I'm sorry," I apologized, feeling the urgent need to right all of my wrongs.

"For what?"

"Doug...he's your husband, right?"

"How do you know my husband?"

Before I could answer, Paula looked up—both of us hearing soft footsteps coming down the hallway. "She's comin'," she whispered. "She...she," Paula pointed to the shadow approaching. "She promised me free drugs if I did it...I...I...just wanted to get high."

"Bitch, what the fuck are you doin'? Pick up the got damn gun and finish her off." Tink said, looking down at me and decked out in an all-black hooded jumpsuit. "Finish her off if you want the rest of these." She held out her hand and opened it, revealing a small bag of purple pills.

Paula's eyes widened and her mouth watered as she eyed the small, purple mound of drugs in the palm of Tink's hand. She started scratching her arms and darting her eyes back and forth at me and then the rocks...at the rocks and then me...back and forth until she picked the gun up—her addiction outweighing her compassion. There were a million thoughts racing through my mind, mainly the fact that I had been shot over a nigga that I didn't even fuck—black ass Dameon, who was still M.I.A since the night I left him unconscious at the Courtyard.

Tink's lips were moving. She was talking shit, but I couldn't hear a word she was saying because of the ringing in my ears from the loud gunshot. Paula had pulled the trigger.

Shonni

Chapter 30

The car swerved into the left-hand lane. *Oh, shit!* I jerked the car back onto the right side of the road. I had polished off the entire bottle of Vodka. I was fucked up. *Lights-out blasted.* It was my first mistake of the night, breaking my own rule and stepping outside of my unit with my senses impaired. But, going into battle with Guy, I needed a few drinks to calm my damn nerves. They had me jumping and shaking and shit like I had Tourette's. However, thanks to all of the *al-al-al-alcohol* that I had consumed, my nerves had been put to rest and I was feeling *grrrrreat!*

My second mistake of the night was driving under the influence. The flashing blue lights in my rearview mirror reiterated the fact. *Shit!* I slowed down and pulled over. Two cops—one old and white and the other young and black—approached the car.

"Step out of the car."

"Don't you know how to say please? And aren't you suppose to ask me for my license and registration first?" I asked, not too totally fucked up that I had forgotten my rights. I motioned to open the glove compartment.

"Reach for the glove compartment again and I will be inclined to believe that you are reaching for a weapon and who knows what that might lead me to do."

Old... dirty...bastard. Instantly, I knew that his white ass was a dirty cop amongst other things. *Racist prick.* I made eye contact with the black officer.

"So, you just gone stand there and let him threaten me like that?" He put his head down with the quickness. "Nigga, whose team are you on? Man that's fucked-up." He didn't say shit as his partner continued to harass me.

"I'm not goin' to tell you again. Step out of the car."

I DO NOT have time for this shit, I thought, unbuckling my seatbelt. It was a quarter till ten. I had fifteen minutes to make it back to the trap house to meet up with him, Heedy and the rest of their camp to go over the plan to take down Guy before the takedown went down.

I opened the door and stumbled out of the car—a sure sign that my alcohol blood level was way over the legal limit. There was no need for a breathalyzer, for me to walk the line or stand on one foot and try to touch my nose simultaneously. It was clear I was drunk as hell and about to be arrested and hauled off to jail on a DUI charge.

"Turn around," the dirty cop ordered. As I did, he forcefully bent me over onto the hood of my car, raising up the trench coat that I had on and exposing my apple-shaped ass. "This one here is a real freak...must be my lucky day." My baring it all was all a part of the plan—to hypnotize the enemy with my God-given assets and hidden talents, setting up the perfect opportunity for Man-Man and his camp to make their move.

As usual, I was looking good enough to eat. Even intoxicated, I had applied my make-up flawlessly.

As the prick-of-a-cop pushed my head further down towards the hood of my car, heat from the engine warmed my cheek. His bitch-ass partner did nothing while he groped my body. I tried to fight him back, but I was unsuccessful; he was too strong for me to overtake. I heard him unzip his pants, slipping his little dick through the hole of his boxers. Just as he was about to stick the tip of his one-eyed-baby snake in my ass, his radio went off.

"187...187," the dispatcher ranted off the police code for gunshots Ki-Ki. "187 in East Bridge Projects. All units in the area respond...all units in the area respond."

"Got damn it!" He released his hold on me and as he did, I turned around and did the despicable. I spit in his face. The wad of phlegm landed in the corner of his left eye.

"You oreo!" He yelled, chasing after me as I ran to the other side of my car. We played a game of cat and mouse until his radio buzzed again.

"All units in the area respond to East Bridge…all units."

"Let's just go, Man," the young black officer finally found the nerve say something.

They hopped in their police cruiser and sped away. I hopped in the driver's seat and did the same, swerving in and out of my lane—all the way to my destination.

* * *

The car spun around and came to a screeching halt. I jumped out of the car and raced down the alley leading to the back door of the trap house.

"You late," Dollar said and opened the heavy steel door like it was lighter than a feather.

"I know," I said, entering the trap house.

Manson, Heedy and an army of niggas—pulled from their duties on the corner—surrounded one of the pool tables in the lounge area of the trap house. *I bet a lot of broads been man handled on this sucker,* I thought, sauntering up to the pool table to join them.

Man-Man looked at me and smirked. "We doin' this shit for you and you comin' up in here late."

"I got pulled over and secondly...you're doin' this to pad your pockets. I know how you get down...money over everything. I'm here now."

Spread out in the middle of the pool table were the blueprints to the Dupont Hotel; mainly the area surrounding the suite Guy was residing in where the transaction—the tradeoff of cash for Power—was scheduled to go down.

Manson marked the blueprints with large red X's, indicating the locations around the hotel where he wanted niggas to post up and be on the lookout. "Izzo, I want you right here. Pop, I want you right here. E, I want you right here. Air out anything you see movin'...even your own shadow."

"Solid," Izzo said.

"Shonni, you know what to do?"

I nodded my head. "I got it."

Heedy, you goin' in with me, Shonni, and Dollar."

"Cool."

"Y'all niggas ready?"

"Ready!" The entire camp, including me, responded.

"It's a go," Manson said, leading the way.

* * *

Masked behind the tint of a motorcade of black vehicles, we arrived at the Dupont Hotel. Several valet attendants rushed Manson's Mercedes Maybach 62S.

"No thanks," he, stepping out of the ultra-luxurious vehicle. *Those massaging seats are what's up,* I thought as I stepped out of the car behind him, reluctant to leave such luxurious accommodations. "My man'z is just droppin' us off," he told the valet attendant whose dream of getting a big tip had just been crushed. "Nigga," Man-Man turned to a trap boy, who was lucky to be driving the Maybach.
"Be back out here in forty-five minutes with the engine runnin'…"

"Man-Man, I got you my nigga."

Heedy, Dollar and I trailed Manson through the revolving doors of the hotel as the rest of the goons followed the instructions he gave earlier.

Making our way through the vast hotel, Dollar carried two shiny silver briefcases in each of his hands. Along the way, we stopped in the Garden. Buried deep into the soil of a massive clay pot—home to one of the garden's towering plants—were two black duffle bags containing enough arsenal for an all-out war. Some broads from Manson's camp had planted the duffle bags earlier. *Smart move,* I thought. After retrieving them, we slipped into a nearby empty banquet room where he disbursed the steel as he saw fit. Izzo, Pop, E and the others vanished into their positions while Manson, Heedy, Dollar and I headed to the suite.

"I don't know why the fuck you pattin' us down. You know we packin'. Why the fuck would we come up here with millions of dollars in cash with no got damn heat?" Manson verbally assaulted Guy's bodyguard.

"Just need to see what you got."

Man-Man lifted up his jean leg, exposing the .45 strapped to his ankle and then turned around, lifting up his black button-up to reveal the .9mm tucked in the waistband of his Polo boxers and resting against the small of his back. Everyone else showed what they were strapped with as well, we were escorted through the suite and into the dining room; an area of the suite that I was all too familiar with. Instead of the array of foreign delicacies and platters of coke that had once rested in the middle of the dining room table, there were ten shiny silver briefcases—just like the two Dollar had in his hands—open and filled with huge Zip-Loc bags of Power; six lining each side of the table.

"Manson my nigga" Guy came walking into the room with his Partner and all of the members of the "delegation" behind him—all of them armed.

"Haitian Guy" The two shook hands.

"You got my money?"

Guy and his people were on one side of the table and we were on the other.

"It's all here," Manson gestured for Heedy to set the briefcases on the table and open them up. "I got somethin' else for you tonight too…somethin' real special." Man-Man grinned.

I unknotted the belt on the trench coat that I was wearing and let it sink to the floor. Except for the strappy Jimmy Choo's on my feet, I stood unclothed—nothing that the delegation hadn't seen before. *Nothin' yet.* Like a snake, I slithered my way onto the table; near the spot where I was raped and dead smack in front of Guy. I spread my thighs open, licked my fingers and guided them down to my pussy—playing with my clit before pulling out a long string of pearls and electrifying the delegation. I could only make out the "oooohhh's" and the "awwwhhh's" as they chatted in French. Like a cowboy capturing cattle, I swung the pearls around Guy's neck and pulled him in closer to the table. *I should have choked his ass right then and there.* I loosened the drawstring on the lounging pants that he had on, pulled out his small dick, flipped over, tilted my head down off the table and gobbled his shit up. His dick throbbed in my mouth as I sucked the life out of it. All eyes were on me—just as planned. Several members of the delegation placed their weapons on the table and formed a single-file line behind Guy, hoping to get served.

Just as he was about to explode in my mouth, his bodyguard came waltzing into the dining room. A Mexican nigga, dressed in a white shirt and black pants, followed behind him—pushing a room service cart.

"Boss, did you order room…"

"Every-fuckin'-body freeze! Police! I said freeze!" The Mexican nigga pulled a gun from under a sterling silver food tray that was on the cart while a sea of agents rushed into the suite.

"Man, fuck this!" Manson was on some renegade shit. He eyed his crew as he reached for his .9mm. In a matter of seconds, bullets were flying—in and from every direction.

"Ugh!" I gasped as I saw a bullet enter and exit Heedy's forehead. He dropped to the floor instantly.

"Oh, shit!" Dollar said, dodging a bullet and ducking underneath the table. Seconds later, he was hit in the chest.

"Heedy!" I screamed, still lying on my back on the table—not yet scathed.

Manson was still blasting off bullets, using one of the briefcases as a shield. After striking a few members of the "delegation" down and some of the narcotic agents, Pop took several bullets to his body. He crashed onto the floor and I could have sworn the earth trembled. Guy took a bullet to the temple courtesy of

Man-Man.   When the smoked cleared, there was only one man standing- Manson.

"I except escaped from the zoo huh," He said with the gun directed to my head.

"Wait, I was just playing." *I know this nigga wasn't going to kill me.* "I loved you Manson…"

"Love on these…" He squeezed the trigger and sprayed my body with an entire round of bullets from his .45. They entered my flesh and my body *thudded* to the floor. Man-Man closed and locked all of the briefcases on the table and I watched as Izzo and E bum rushed the suite and helped Manson carry out all of the briefcases—the money and the drugs. Manson had gotten away with it all and without one war wound.

I closed my eyes, thinking that my third mistake of the night was trusting that Manson had my back. I thought about what Ms. Vett said about crossing him and then about my kids; a single tear was shed for them before I drifted into an eternal sleep.

Carly

Chapter 31

Ki-Ki came cussing and screaming out of her unit—ready to kill somebody. She had on a long, cotton robe with tiny sailboats printed on it and wearing a pair of her cherished bootie socks with some flip flops.

"Who the hell out here doin' all that damn shootin'," she said, adjusting the scarf wrapped around her head. "The cops ain't never around when you need them. I ain't heard one siren," she said, coming towards me as I was stepping outside of my unit to go next door to Asha's for some salt and pepper.

"Ki-Ki, now you know somebody be shootin' every other day in projects...you should be used to it just like the rest of us."

It was sad, but true. I had heard the gunshots while I was putting up the groceries I had been given, but I didn't flinch, duck or even bother taking cover. Synda was in the tub and safe inside; I wasn't worried about anyone else.

"Who the hell gets use to being in the middle of a got damn shootout?"

"I was just sayin' you know how they do around here…always shootin' some shit up. It ain't nothin' new."

Ki-Ki ignored me. Her focus was on Asha's unit door. "Where the hell she go leaving her door open for a stray cat or somethin' worse to get up in there?"

"Nowhere," I said, knowing that Asha would never leave her door open and the farthest she would go and leave it unlocked was just a few feet away to my unit.

As we approached the door, an ill feeling settled in the pit of my stomach. I wasn't for sure if it was a forewarning of what I was about to see or the crime I would commit later.

Light shined from inside of Asha's unit onto her porch through the small gap in the door. "I hope this ain't bout' to be some bullshit," Ki-Ki braced herself.

I motioned to push the door open. "Hold up," Ki-Ki stopped me. "We can't just go up in their unarmed. We need somethin'," she said, looking around and spotting a brick. *This ain't a game of rock, paper, scissors,* I thought to myself as Ki-Ki reached down for the brick—sure that if there was an intruder in Asha's unit, he was packing heat. "Okay," she said, giving me the go ahead.

With caution, I pushed the door wide open, instantly clamping my hands over my mouth at the sight before me. Ki-Ki did the same. From the doorway, Asha's body appeared lifeless.

Screaming, Ki-Ki dropped to her knees. "Fuck-no! no!" She was devastated and probably thinking that if any one of us had to die it shouldn't have been Asha; especially since things where beginning to look up for her. *That's just the way shit went sometimes.*
"Oh my God this is so fucked up,"

There were two shell casing next to Asha's body and a bullet hole in the floor just an inch or so from her head. It was the bullet that missed. The other, I assumed from all of the blood gushing from her midsection, had struck Asha in the stomach. The white t-shirt that she was wearing had been dyed red by her own blood and her hands were also covered in blood from her touching her wound. I could see her chest heaving up and down and I could hear her faintly gasp for air every few seconds. She hadn't passed yet. *Thank you...thank you.* I wasn't for sure who I was thanking, but I said it—looking up. I had witnessed the murders of Cream, Pop and the twins, was facing my own mortality and was about to try and comfort my best friend during what could possibly be the last few moments of her life. Death was all around me.

I sat on the floor next to Asha, taking her in my arms as her blood seeped into my own shirt; wiping away her tears as I held back mine. We fought each other, but that was irrelevant now.

"Asha," I said, rocking her back and forth in my arms. "Stay awake for me, okay. Open your eyes." I gently nudged her face. "Open your eyes, Asha." I waited a few seconds. She didn't respond. *Fuck!* But she was still breathing scarcely.

Asha had serviced a lot of tricks and had had her run-ins with their significant others. But they always found her down on the Ave, unknowing of where she lived. Whoever attacked her, knew her—I was sure of that, and I had a gut feeling about who she was. This was clearly a case of a-bitch-paying-another-bitch-back; revenge. Everybody knew that Tink was ill about what Jella had told her about seeing Dameon and Asha together.

"I'm goin' to ask you a question. Squeeze my hand if the answer is yes." I locked hands with her. "Did Tink do this to you?" Seconds passed. I asked again. "Asha, did Tink shoot you? You gotta give me somethin'. Please, Asha...give me somethin'." I felt the pressure of Asha's fingers pushing down on mine. "Good...good." *That bitch. Oh, it's goin' down and so is Jael's.* I was planning on burning his salon all the way down...with him in it.

I hugged Asha tighter. "Now...listen to me. It's not your time." I wiped the tears that I could no longer hold back from my eyes with the back of my arm, smearing blood all over my face. "You hear me, Asha? It's not your time."

* * *

Asha's unit was taped off in crime scene tape and crawling with police officers, EMTs and even a few firefighters who had responded to the call. The entire scene was reminiscent of an episode of Law & Order—when the Victim's body is discovered. The only difference was that the scene unraveling inside of Asha's unit was real.

As if a block concert was taking place, the street was crowded with onlookers. Everyone had emerged from their units and lined the street to see what was going on. Ms. Vett was still crying, leaned up against a police cruiser while Dosha comforted and promised her that everything was going to be okay...she hoped. Asha was closer to Ms. Vett than Shonni and I. Even before Asha's aunt had been murdered, Asha sought refuge in Ms. Vett's motherly nature - something that her aunt, Lynn, lacked. Over the years, they had truly formed somewhat of a mother-daughter bond on the low. Ms. Vett was taking the incident hard.

Police officers were going door to door, asking questions. I had managed to slip away from the scene without being questioned and without offering up any information. I suppose I was good at that—not offering up information. But, I wasn't keeping the identity of Asha's killer a secret because I was scared that she would attack me as in the case of Cream, Pop and the twins' killers. My goal was to get to Tink before the police did. *They'll find her ass...burnt to a got damn crisp.*

I returned to my unit, painted in blood; not wanting to hear the EMTs pronounce Asha dead or watch them roll her out in a body bag on a stretcher. I had seen enough in the last few weeks; more than any pairs of eyes should have to witness.

Upon returning to my unit, my intentions were to get Synda and take her over to Ki-Ki's with Dream and the kids. And then to hit up Shonni; I needed a ride and a gun. *A bat just wouldn't do...not up against a bullet.* I figured the only other things I needed were some kerosene and a pack of matches. I was about to commit two crimes; murder and arson.

But, when I turned the doorknob and entered my unit, my heart stopped. It turned cold as I listened to the grunts and moans of a grown man...amid my daughter's cries for help. This was the man...the shadow that I had sensed hovering over me lately. He had been watching me and waiting for the perfect opportunity to do the despicable...the unthinkable— not to me but to my daughter.

Any good mother would have raced to her daughter's side in that moment, fighting the child molester off. But, I wasn't a good mother. I had been a horrible mother; always saying I wanted to be a better mother but never following through. And I didn't want to be a good mother anymore. I wanted to be a great one and in my mind, in that moment, I did what I thought any great mother would do. I headed to the kitchen.

Several thoughts raced through my mind as I blamed myself for the torture Synda was enduring. *I should have locked the door. I shouldn't have left her here by herself...even if I did think I was just goin' to be gone a few minutes. I should have gotten a real job...a gig that paid enough for me to live somewhere nice. I should have never moved into the projects...no child should live here...in poverty...amongst crime...havin' to dodge bullets...havin' to dodge child molesters.*

I never regretted having Synda. She brought my joy and now I had brought her pain.

My grandmother—awful in her own right—did make me, my sister and brother attend Sunday school on occasion. I remember one class in which our Sunday school teacher told us that we needed to be good little boys and girls because if we didn't our future children would bear the grunt of our sins. I'm sure she had taken whatever scripture it was out of context, but it scared us. At least for that Sunday morning it did, but I thought about it and it made sense. Synda had not inherited my sins, but she was suffering from them. What was happening to Synda was my fault and there was only one thing that I could do to rectify the situation; to be deemed a great mother.

I didn't have much in the likes of pots and pans or dishes, but I had a selection of knives—the set Dream had given to me as a housewarming gift when I moved into my own unit. I grabbed the one with the biggest handle; the biggest blade. And I walked into to the biggest nightmare of my life...my eight-year-old daughter being sexually assaulted. I walked towards the grunts, towards the moans, towards the cries.

He hadn't bothered taking her into her bedroom or mine. He had snatched her out of the tub and proceeded to take away her innocence on the bathroom floor. With each pump, he groaned. With each stroke, he moaned. He didn't sense me behind him—too occupied with raping my daughter. His back was infected with sores—those identical to the lesions that were forming on my body.

As if I was about to go up and serve a volleyball, I lifted my hand high in the air and brought it down hard, stabbing my daughter's attacker in the middle of his back. I stabbed him over and over again. He was dead after the fifteenth stab wound or so and had rolled off of Synda. I picked her up from off of the wet, sod and blood filled floor and carried her into her bedroom, wrapping her shivering and cold body in her favorite Hello Kitty blanket. She was crying and bleeding some, but she was conscious.

I returned to the bathroom to finish what I had started. *A chain saw. That's what I need,* I remembered thinking. I did my best without one, chopping Amber's father up into as many pieces as I could with a kitchen knife. *For Synda and Amber.*

Blood was everywhere. On the walls, soaked into the peach-colored rugs I had purchased on sale from Wal-Mart and covering the toilet seat. The roll of tissue setting on top of the tank of the toilet was even spotted with blood. His blood. Asha's blood. Synda's blood.

There was a knock on my door. Without cleaning myself up and with the knife still in my hand, I went to answer it, leaving a bloody trail from the bathroom to the front door.

"Ma'am, we just…," the officer started and abruptly stopped what I was sure to be a long line of questioning about what happened to Asha. I didn't recognize him or his partner—two on the force that I hadn't previously crossed paths with. They looked horrified. *Maybe it's all the blood.*

𝕬𝕤𝕳𝕒

𝕰𝕡𝕚𝕝𝕠𝕘𝕦𝕖

The church was packed to capacity, standing room only for the late comers. I spotted Ms. Vett on the front pew. She was already crying, blowing snot into a wad of Kleenex. Seeing her cry brought back the memory of the day we laid Shonni, and Heedy to rest. We had all come together as a community to pay our respects to them and the others who had lost their lives during Man-Man's drug deal gone bad. From the news reports, it was a total massacre. Several narcotic agents had also lost their lives amongst the dead from Man-Man and Guy's camps. It had indeed been a bloody night inside and outside of the Bridges.

Shonni must have thought things were going to go bad. She left a letter with Ms. Vett with her mother's information. Shonni's mom came and got her grandchildren and exposed Neil. Needless to say he is no longer mayor. He is actually facing statutory rape charges and a large civil suit.

I, of course, had survived Tink and Paula's attack on my life. I walked away without any permanent damage. Paula eventually turned herself in, escorted to the police station by her husband. They, of course, divorced. And Tink had skipped town. She was on the run. *Her ass is looney*, I thought, refusing to think about her any further. *Not today.*

I peeked through the church doors again. Ki-Ki was still crying. *She's gone to have to stop all of that.* It was my wedding day; a joyous occasion. I had been adamant about not crying, but the sight of Synda looking so beautiful in her dress and smiling after all that she had been through brought me to tears. She was standing near the altar, fiddling with the white, wicker flower basket in her hands. AJ, Dream's now two-year-old son, was next to her—seated in the red wagon he was rolled down the aisle in. Both of them looked adorable. *Two down, four to go*, I thought—thinking about the years Synda had left, in which, she had to be tested for HIV every six months. So far, the four tests she had taken had come back negative. *Nothin' but the grace of God.* After Carly was arrested for murdering Amber's father, she stayed with Ms. Vett until I recuperated. There was no way I was going to let her become a ward of the state. I filed for legal guardianship over her and she now lived with Blair and I. She was doing excellent in school; an A-student and we continued to make her go see a therapist twice a week even though she seemed to be coping well with everything that had happened to her and with her mother's passing.

Carly had succumbed to AIDS in the mental ward. She had refused treatment, believing that she'd go when it was her time. Up until her death, I had taken Synda to visit her every month. She had lived to see Synda turn nine and had left letters for me to give Synda to read on other monumental days and moments in her life: the day she started her period, her first dance, her first date, her high school graduation, her eighteenth birthday, first day of college and her wedding day. She also left a list of all of the names of the men she could remember sleeping with instructions to send it to Porter Center Health Department. I thanked God daily that the onetime Cream didn't use a Condom-I too wasn't affected.

According to the final coroner's report, Carly had stabbed Amber's father a total of one hundred and-eight times—that was the total stab wounds that could be identified on the parts of his body that Carly hadn't attempted to chop up with the kitchen knife she had used to kill him. Her lawyer ruled mentally insane, but because she had stopped to take Synda into her room and then returned to mutilate his body further, the judge agreed and she was committed to the state hospital. And when Carly was initially arrested, she was given one phone call. She called Crime

Stoppers—from jail. I shook my head and laughed. She gave the police all of the information they needed to arrest the men –who had killed Cream, Pop & the twins. In return, she was given the $15,000 reward that Blair and I used to establish a college fund for Synda.

"You okay?" Pam signed to me.

"Yes." I nodded as she dabbed the tears from the corners of my eye.

"You can't be messin' up your make-up."

I finished the program with honors. I was working towards a bachelor's degree in nursing I also helped Pam run the program when I wasn't in class. Never before in my life had I ever considered myself blessed, but that's the only word that truly described my life.

And the two words that best described Blair coming into my life were *God sent;* not because he was fine and rich, but because he was my soul mate— the person who came into my life and inspired me to be a better woman. *Life...life is good.*

"You ready?" Pam asked. I nodded yes as she signaled the ushers to open the church doors.

I walked down the aisle, the happiest I had ever been in my life. I was determined to instill in Synda that she could be anything that she wanted to be in life; that nothing or no one could hold her back but herself.

The End

So Real You Feel You Lived It!

Street Knowledge Publishing LLC
1902-B Maryland Ave
Wilmington, DE 19805
TOLL FREE: **1.888.401.1114**
www.streetknowledgepublishing.com

Date: _____

Purchaser _____

Mailing Address _____

City _____ State _____ Zip Code _____

Qty.	ISB Number	Title of Book	Price Each	Total
	978-0-9822515-6-0	Bloody Money	$15.00	
	978-0-9822515-9-1	Bloody Money 2	$15.00	
	978-0-9799556-4-8	Bloody Money 3	$15.00	
	978-0-9799556-0-0	Tommy Good story	$15.00	
	978-0-9822515-0-8	Tommy Good Story II	$15.00	
	978-0-9746199-1-0	Me & My Girls	$15.00	
	978-0-9746199-0-3	Cash Ave	$15.00	
	978-0-9822515-1-5	Merry F$$kin' Xmas	$15.00	
	978-0-9799556-0-7	A Day After Forever	$15.00	
	978-0-9822515-3-9	A Day After Forever 2	$15.00	
	978-0-9746199-6-5	Don't Mix the Bitter with the Sweet	$15.00	
	978-0-9799556-9-3	Playing For Keeps	$15.00	
	978-0-9799556-3-1	Pain Freak	$15.00	
	978-0-9799556-5-5	Dipped Up	$15.00	
	978-0-9799556-6-2	No Love No Pain	$15.00	
	978-0-9746199-4-1	Dopesick	$15.00	
	978-0-9799556-7-9	Lust, Love & Lies	$15.00	
	978-0-9746199-7-2	The Queen of New York	$15.00	
	978-0-9746199-8-9	Sin 4 Life	$15.00	
	978-0-9822515-4-6	A Little More Sin	$15.00	
	978-0-9746199-5-8	The Hunger	$15.00	
	978-0-9746199-3-4	Money Grip	$15.00	
	978-0-9822515-7-7	Young Rich and Dangerous	$15.00	
	978-1-944151-26-3	Street Victims	$15.00	
	978-1-944151-28-7	Street Victims II	$15.00	
	978-1-944151-30-3	Street Victimes III	$15.00	
	978-1-944151-32-4	A Small Wonder	$15.00	
	978-1-944151-45-4	Coup De Grace	$15.00	
	978-1-944151-47-8	Burton Boys (May 2017)	$15.00	
	978-1-944151-56-0	Burton Boys 2	$15.00	
	978-1-944151-58-4	Burton Boys 3	$15.00	
	978-1-944151-00-3	Dirty Living	$15.00	
	978-1-944151-65-2	Watch What You Say	$15.00	
		Total Books Ordered	Quantity	
			Subtotal	

SHIPPING/HANDLING (Via U.S. Priority Mail)
$7.20 for 1st book, $2.00 for each additional book
Institutional Check & Money Orders ONLY
(No Personal Checks Accepted)

Shipping
Total

Total $ _____

Street Knowledge Publishing LLC
1902-B Maryland Ave
Wilmington, DE 19805
TOLL FREE: **1.888.401.1114**
www.streetknowledgepublishing.com

Date: _____

Purchaser _____

Mailing Address _____

City _____ State _____ Zip Code _____

Qty.	ISB Number	Title of Book	Author	Price Each	Total
	Butterfly Collection				
		Beautiful Demise	K.D. Harris	$13.99	
		Scarred	K.D. Harris	$13.99	
		Pressure (Coming April 2017)	K.D. Harris	$13.99	
		Dying to Fit In (Coming June 2017)	K.D. Harris	$13.99	
		Legacy (Coming August 2017)	K.D. Harris	$13.99	
		Classy Clique (Coming Sept. 2017)	K.D. Harris	$13.99	
		Caged Secrets (Coming Nov. 2017)	K.D. Harris	$13.99	
		Messy Media (Coming Dec. 2017)	K.D. Harris	$13.99	
	SKP Erotica				
	978-1-944151-04-1	Beyond Measure	K.D. Harris	$15.00	
	978-1-944151-06-5	Beyond Measure II	K.D. Harris	$15.00	
	978-1-944151-62-1	Beyond Measure III (April 2017)	K.D. Harris	$15.00	
	978-1-944151-08-9	The Games We Play	K.D. Harris	$15.00	
	978-1-944151-02-7	For The Love Of It	K.D. Harris	$15.00	
	Eric B Crime Novels				
	978-1-944151-20-1	That Was Dirty	Wasiim	$15.00	
	978-1-944151-22-5	It Gets Dirtier	Wasiim	$15.00	
	978-1-944151-24-9	As Dirty As It Gets	Wasiim	$15.00	
	978-0-9799556-8-6	Money and Murder	Fred Brown	$15.00	
	978-1-944151-35-5	Money and Murder II	Fred Brown	$15.00	
	978-1-944151-39-7	Money and Murder III	Fred Brown	$15.00	
	978-1-944151-49-2	Scandalous Ties	Jermaine "Ski" Buchanan	$15.00	
	978-1-944151-51-5	Scandalous Ties II	Jermaine "Ski" Buchanan	$15.00	
	978-1-944151-52-2	Scandalous Ties III	Jermaine "Ski" Buchanan	$15.00	
	978-1-944151-55-3	Scandalous Ties IV	Jermaine "Ski" Buchanan	$15.00	
	978-0-9799556-2-4	Courts in the Streets	Kevin Bullock	$15.00	
	978-0-9822515-5-3	Courts in the Streets II	Kevin Bullock	$15.00	
	978-1-944151-43-0	Courts in the Streets III	Kevin Bullock	$15.00	
		Total Books Ordered		Quantity	
				Subtotal	
	SHIPPING/HANDLING (Via U.S. Priority Mail) $7.20 for 1st book, $2.00 for each additional book Institutional Check & Money Orders ONLY (No Personal Checks Accepted)		Shipping	
				Total	
		Total		$	